THE BARKS & BEANS CAFE
MYSTERY SERIES

ICED OVER

THE BARKS AND BEANS CAFE MYSTERY
SERIES: BOOK 2

HEATHER DAY GILBERT

FROM THE BACK COVER

Welcome to the Barks & Beans Cafe, a quaint place where folks pet shelter dogs while enjoying a cup of java...and where murder sometimes pays a visit.

Black Friday turns fatal when an armored security truck hits an icy patch and runs over an embankment near the cafe. With one driver dead and the other in a coma, police are baffled by the discovery that $500,000 is missing from the truck's cache.

When strangers show up at Barks & Beans asking nosy questions about a young cafe employee, Macy's mama bear instincts kick in. She can't ignore what her gut is telling her—that things aren't all they seem on the surface—and with a little help from her brother, Bo, and her Great Dane, Coal, Macy follows up on a few leads of her own. But if the ruthless thief beats her to the stash, the thin ice she's been skating on might just crack.

Join siblings Macy and Bo Hatfield as they sniff out crimes in their hometown...with plenty of dogs along for the ride! The Barks & Beans Cafe cozy mystery series features a small town, an amateur sleuth, and no swearing or graphic scenes. Find all the books at heatherdaygilbert.com!

The Barks & Beans Cafe series in order:
   Book 1: No Filter
   Book 2: Iced Over
   Book 3: Fair Trade

Dedicated to my mother in law Jane Gilbert, who surprised us all by slipping home to heaven this year. You were a constant encouragement and friend to me. You'll never be forgotten.

1

IF EVER THERE were a perfect anchor for our Thanksgiving table, it was Great Aunt Athaleen's blue Carnival glass bowl. Cradling its weighty base, I carefully set it on the runner I'd smoothed out earlier. Thanksgiving this year would be so different with Auntie A gone, but I took a moment to be grateful my brother Boaz and I would be celebrating it here in the family home.

The truth was, I owed Bo for talking me into moving back to our hometown in Lewisburg, West Virginia. He was the one who'd renovated the front of Auntie A's house into a cafe and invited me to live in the back half.

He'd lured me in with dogs, of course. I ran the "Barks" half of the Barks & Beans Cafe, and Bo ran the cafe section. With my dog instincts and his coffee bean connections, it had turned out to be the perfect match. The cafe had only been open since September, but we'd already had to hire another employee just to keep up with business.

My black Great Dane, Coal, shot me a polite and somewhat apologetic look from his pillow in the living room.

The moment I'd started bustling around the table, he'd sat back on his haunches and made a rather Herculean effort to ignore me. His casual act didn't fool me. We both knew that if I took the time to set the table, food would show up soon—most likely arriving with Bo, who was the cook in the family.

I'd surprised myself, though, by giving into a wild urge to replicate Auntie A's mashed potatoes for the Thanksgiving meal. After several failed attempts, I'd finally gotten my potatoes mashed to perfection, blended with just enough milk, salt and pepper, and butter. I had a bowl of potatoes sitting in the microwave, waiting for the guests to arrive, at which point I'd heat them and drown them in even more butter.

To expand upon my mashed potato offering this Thanksgiving, I'd made yeast rolls and warmed a couple of cans of Auntie A's canned applesauce. The rolls were turning a lovely golden brown, and the house smelled of apples, cinnamon, and bread—a heady combination that seemed just right.

Thankfully, Bo was handling the turkey, as well as the stuffing and gravy. Our pet shelter owner friend, Summer Adkins, was bringing a tossed salad and a couple of pies for dessert. Bo and I had agreed that we needed to invite a third party, simply because we'd celebrated the holiday for so many years with the two of us and Auntie A. We were used to cooking for three.

Something thudded against my back door.

"Let me in!" Bo's hands were likely too full to ring the doorbell, which was just as well since it tended to send Coal into a frenzy.

"Coming!" I shot a look at Coal, who continued to feign indifference by focusing on a ladybug crawling on the wall. I couldn't help but chuckle. "Stay," I commanded, although he was well-trained enough that he didn't even need me to say it.

He already knew it was Bo, and that no matter how big and intimidating my brother looked, he was *not* to bark at him.

Coal instinctively got a fact some people failed to pick up on—you cross my brother, you cross me. And my loyal dog would rather roll over and die than to cross me.

Bo looked spiffy in his plaid poplin shirt with the sleeves rolled up. He'd trimmed his red beard and smelled fresh, like he'd just showered. He handed me the long basket that held a couple of hot dishes, then returned to the car, presumably for the turkey roasting pan. I headed to the kitchen and deposited the basket on the counter, then opened the screen door for Bo.

All this was done without the exchange of a single word. Sometimes I marveled at our strong sibling connection, although I knew ours was forged in steel the moment our parents had died. I was only two at the time, and Bo was six. Outside of Auntie A, who'd adopted us soon after, we were all we had left.

"Something smells great," he said.

I lapped up his uncommon praise for my cooking. "Thanks. And thanks for making the turkey. You're the only one who can get that right."

A light voice carried into the house. "I don't know about that," Summer said, her tiered skirt flowing down to her shoes. "I make a pretty mean bird. Try me next year."

Summer had recently abandoned her fling with purple hair and had gotten it dyed back to its natural dark honey blonde. Today she'd braided it, securing the braids in a double loop around her head.

I took in her colorful blue and red skirt, white blouse, and perfectly pinned braids. "Anyone ever tell you that you look like a Swedish milkmaid?" I asked.

Summer grinned. "Give me that rockin' apron so I can complete the effect."

I glanced down at the red gingham ruffled apron tied around my waist. "Touché," I said, taking the giant wooden salad bowl from her and placing it on the table. Summer had finally loosened up around us, and we always had a fun time.

"How's your kitty doing?" Summer asked Bo.

A smile spread across Bo's face. Last month, Summer and I had surmised that since Bo wasn't crazy about dogs, he might be a cat person, so we had contrived to introduce Bo to a foster kitten Summer needed to place. One day when Summer dropped the shelter dogs off at the cafe, she'd pulled the calico kitten from her pocket, and just as we'd suspected, Bo hadn't been able to resist the tiny kitten's purrs. Bo had named her Stormy because she was like a storm in a teacup. Wild as she was, Stormy was also adorable, right down to her long, soft hair and startlingly green eyes.

"She's getting into trouble," he said. "I bought her *two* fancy cat towers, but where does she spend all her time? In an old box."

"Typical cat," Summer said. She turned to me. "And how does she get along with your big brute of a dog? I wondered how a Dane would do with such a runt of a kitten."

"Surprisingly well," I said. "He watches her every move, but if he tries to get close, she swipes at him and hisses."

Bo chuckled. "That kitten has the personality of a mountain lion. I don't think she's afraid of anything." His cell phone rang, so he moseyed off down the hall to answer it. I hoped his ex-fiancée, Tara, wasn't checking in for the holiday. Bo had told me he wasn't hung up on her anymore, but I wasn't so sure.

"Make yourself at home while I putter around with the last minute stuff," I told Summer, hoping Bo would carve the turkey soon. Everything else was nearly ready.

She wandered around, finally picking up a photo album. She squealed with delight and pointed to a photo. "You two were adorable! Look at your fluffy hair—it's the same color as a fuzzy peach. And Bo's haircut!"

Bo walked in. "Auntie A insisted on cutting it herself," he said. "I'll have you know those super short bangs were ahead of their time."

"You would've fit right in with my Mennonite brothers," Summer said.

"You have brothers?" I asked, astonished.

She closed the photo album. "I do. Four of them. But I don't see them anymore. Not since I left."

I set out the salad dressings. "Sisters, too?"

Summer shook her head and walked my way. "Nope, like you, I was only blessed with brothers."

Bo retrieved one of Auntie A's large yellow flowered china dishes and began carving the turkey onto it. "Hey, sis, I just got a call from Dylan. I hope you don't mind, but I asked if he wanted to drop in today. He said he's with his family right now, but he could stop in for dessert."

I continued placing rolls in a basket. "Uh, sure."

Dylan Butler was a local art gallery owner who'd helped Bo select artwork for the interior of Barks & Beans. I'd gone on a couple of dates with him, but I wasn't really ready to pursue a relationship with anyone yet, even though my divorce from Jake had been finalized earlier this year.

The only reason our divorce had been finalized so quickly was because I'd been able to file in West Virginia. Thankfully, at the time we got married, I hadn't yet shifted my residency to South Carolina. If I'd had to divorce in South Carolina, I would *still* be married, since I'd have to wait for a full year of separation to play out before I could even file the divorce papers on that cheating toot.

Yes, West Virginia had always treated me well.

I had nothing against Dylan. We had a lot in common,

since I'd minored in art history in college, so we always had good conversations. He could only add to our afternoon meal. "I'm glad you asked him," I said, motioning Bo and Summer over to the table.

As they pulled out their chairs, I dropped a couple of doggie treats on the floor in front of Coal and washed my hands before settling at the table myself. Bo asked the blessing, getting a little choked up as he spoke of how Auntie A would be proud we were carrying on the tradition of a Hatfield holiday meal in her house.

I tried to reel my thoughts in from drifting toward last Christmas, when I was still with Jake the Snake and Auntie A could no longer hide her late-stage ovarian cancer. It had been a horrible way to start a new year, and things had only slid downhill from there until I'd moved home this summer.

I hoped and prayed we were coming up on one of the best years yet for Bo and me. I peeked around at Summer, Bo, and Coal, and knew that if nothing else, I was exactly where I was supposed to be right now. And that felt like enough.

2

Black Friday—which also happened to be my day off—started off with a bang. Not only did I sleep in until eleven, but I also devoured the last piece of Summer's caramel pecan pie as my decadent and utterly satisfying late breakfast. I dropped onto the couch in my soft PJs, only to jerk my head back as Coal tried to shove his massive face toward my own.

"No treats," I said. "Get down."

My muscular dog obeyed, but his upturned triangular ears didn't relax. They were perpetually on the alert because they'd been clipped as a puppy. Summer and I figured Coal was intended to be a show dog, but something must've fallen through since his previous owner, Gerard Fontaine, had never showed or even bred him. In fact, he'd had him neutered. The vet looked over the paperwork and concluded that Coal didn't have any genetic abnormalities, so she speculated his behavior might've changed and Gerard didn't feel he could handle him as a stud dog.

I still wondered what was going through Gerard's head when he bought Coal as a puppy, but I'd never know. Gerard had been murdered not long ago, and while it was a brutal death, I was extremely grateful his dog had wound up going into the shelter, where Summer put a bug in my ear about him. Coal had never showed any behavioral issues with me.

I didn't have to be at the cafe today because our new girl, Bristol Goddard, was working in the dog room today.

Bristol was a sweet twenty-two year old who was perfectly comfy in her plus-sized frame, always wearing trendy outfits that fit her well. Her round face maintained a kind of innocence and transparency I was immediately drawn to in our interview, probably because Jake had taught me the hard way what duplicity looked like.

Coal had snuggled in at my feet when I realized I'd nodded off watching a gardening show. My morning tea hadn't given me enough caffeine to function today. It was my own fault—I'd stayed up way too late enjoying the retro gaming system Dylan had brought over. Bo had also stayed up late, although around eleven he'd phased out of the gaming and launched into an intense conversation with Summer. By the time we'd called it a night, Dylan and I were hoarse from laughing at the sad game graphics and Summer and Bo were sitting on the couch, closer than I'd ever seen them.

I'd call that a total win of a Thanksgiving.

Glancing outside to see if I needed a coat, I was surprised to see a light layer of snow had fallen in the night. I opened the back door and felt a blast of cold air, so I quickly shut it and donned my hat, gloves, and scarf before taking Coal out. After he did his business in the enclosed back garden and I let him back in the house, I decided I'd rather walk to the cafe's front door than use the communicating door from my hallway into the coffee shop area. It was distracting for customers when the interior door suddenly opened, plus, I didn't like people peering into my section of the three-story house.

As I stepped out the gate onto the sidewalk, my foot nearly slid out from under me. I managed to right myself before glancing down. My foot had pushed back the thin skiff of snow to reveal a layer of ice underneath.

Although the roads had been treated, it would still be downright dangerous for all those Black Friday shoppers since the temperature was well below freezing. My own plan was to grab a strong coffee, then cybershop for all my Christmas deals, but I hoped the in-town shoppers would drop by the cafe for a quick warm-up.

When I had nearly reached the cafe door, someone brushed past me on the front sidewalk, bumping into my arm. The person was wearing a scarf around their face and their gray coat hood was pulled low. I got the impression it was a teen girl, but couldn't be sure. I was about to say "Excuse *you*" when I realized maybe the kid was so bundled up she'd barely registered she'd touched me.

Mildly irritated, I shoved open the cafe door, pausing to breathe in the scent of fresh-brewed coffee. We worked hard to make sure that was the first thing customers smelled. Having several dogs under the same roof could get stinky, but Summer had the shelter dogs bathed before they came to visit, and we had odor-eliminating devices in operation at all times.

Glancing over to see who was working the coffee bar, I noticed one of the Stevens Security truck drivers standing behind the counter. He was very hard to miss. The wide-chested man was in uniform, with a large gun and keyring on his belt and a metal box in his hands. Bo extracted money from the register as the other employees skittered around him to fill the drink orders.

Bristol gave me a wave from the dog area and I waved back, only to realize she wasn't even looking at me. The formidable security guard's face softened a little, and he moved his pinky finger at Bristol. They must know each other, but how, I wondered? He looked twice her age.

I walked over and opened the gate to the doggie room, pleased to see that Bristol had all four dogs under control. The confident girl seemed to be a natural Alpha, so the shelter dogs respected her.

Come to think of it, some part of me must be an Alpha since I also had a knack with dogs, but that certainly wouldn't be the term I'd use to describe myself. More like a blind pushover when it came to choosing men.

"Things going okay?" I asked.

She gathered her long, dark hair into an invisible ponytail before letting it spill back over her shoulders. "Yeah, Summer brought a really mellow group today."

"She seems to be doing that more often. I don't know if the shelter staff are spending more time with the dogs, or if people are just abandoning calmer dogs." I checked myself. "Not to sound harsh, but that's kind of how it goes. They can't really choose which dogs they take in."

"I know what you mean," Bristol said. "It's definitely easier to pair customers with calm dogs, although I've met a few who prefer lively ones."

"*Lively* is quite an understatement with some of these dogs." I winked.

Bristol glanced back to the cafe, where the security truck driver was heading out the door.

"Do you know that guy?" I asked.

"Yeah, he's my uncle," she said. "Uncle Clark. He's the best. He's actually living with my mom and brother and me now, helping Mom pay off the mortgage." A Lab mix dropped a toy on her lap, and she tossed it back to him. She didn't meet my eyes. "I didn't tell you this in my interview, but my dad died young of a heart attack. It was kind of a freak thing, you know? And my brother has polycystic kidney disease, so he's on dialysis three times a week. So my mom works all hours, sitting in homes with the sick and elderly. Uncle Clark stepped up when he found out she wasn't making enough money to keep the house. He stopped renting his apartment and now he pays that rent to Mom so she can cover mortgage payments."

My respect for her uncle Clark just shot to the sky. And for Bristol.

"Is that why you work, too?" I asked gently.

She set to work organizing a toy bin that was already pristine. "Mm-hm," she said, clearing her throat. "For a while I'd thought about getting a graphic design degree at an art college, but things didn't work out in time." She glanced up at me. "I'm so thankful for this job, Miss Hatfield. Mom is too. 'Every little bit helps,' she always says."

As tears sprang to my eyes, it was my turn to pretend to focus on the dogs. This twenty-something was so devoted to her needy family, she'd given up her own dreams to help them out. Auntie A would be so impressed by Bristol's loyalty to her blood kin—something she'd stressed with us. "Everyone else in the world will let you down, but your blood will never turn their backs on you," she'd said. Then she'd add, "And Hatfield blood runs thicker than most."

Bo walked over and peered in. "How's it going over here? Was there a reason you were dropping in, Macy?"

I stood. "Nothing pressing. I just came over to pick up a macchiato since I'm dragging this morning. I'm too lazy to make my own coffee." I grinned. "I was just chatting with Bristol while you were busy."

Bo prepped an extra-frothy cinnamon macchiato for me and we settled at one of the tables. I loved the way he'd furnished the cafe—shoot, I loved that he'd renovated it on his own with no input from me. Interior design stressed me out, and Bo knew that.

Plus, he wasn't suffering for income since he'd cashed out as vice president of the coffee bean distributor Coffee Mass, so he'd hired an interior designer who'd come up with a very natural, relaxed look for Barks & Beans. I tapped at the worn, thick wood table that seemed to harbor all manner of interesting tales. A gas fireplace flickered against the white brick wall and added a cozy feel.

I pointed to the fireplace. "That definitely takes the chill off. I might need to get one for my part of the house."

"That's a good idea, given how drafty it is. I still remember how ice would form *inside* my windowpanes in the wintertime. That's why I had the renovation crew swap those old windows for energy-efficient ones in your section, too." Bo took a sip of his house coffee before dropping his voice. "Say, what's up with Bristol? You both looked kind of teary in there."

I glanced over and could tell that Bristol was still watching me. "We can talk about it later, but it's nothing bad. Let's just say we lucked out when we hired a sweetie like her."

I STOPPED BACK by the cafe around three to chat with Bo about Girl's Day Out, the upcoming town shopping event we were participating in, but he'd just headed out for a late lunch. Business had been steady all morning, despite the icy sidewalks and roads.

I sat down at a table to keep an eye on things while Bo was gone—something I didn't always do, but today was busier. Bo had been training me on how to make some of the coffee drinks, but I only felt confident enough to run the register at this point. That could still help if things suddenly got hectic.

Kylie, our barista with a sprawling dragon tattoo and combat boots, dropped by my table and handed me a pale green macaron with white filling. "Charity made a batch this morning and she wondered what you thought of them. This one is mint."

Charity, our resident baker-slash-barista, never stopped looking for scrumptious new ways to add pounds to the townspeople of Lewisburg. How she found time to experiment in the kitchen, work at Barks & Beans, and foster her four year old grandson was beyond me. The white-haired, cherubic-faced woman gave me a wave from her spot behind the coffee counter.

I took a bite and sighed with delight. "Great day in the morning! That flavor is absolutely perfect. I love the light touch of mint that doesn't overwhelm the vanilla. Not to mention the texture—the cookies are thick, but not heavy, and the filling is so creamy."

I shot Charity a thumbs-up and took another huge bite.

The woman at the table next to me leaned over. "I'll have whatever she's having."

Kylie grinned and headed over to grab another macaron. Once again, Charity had done us all proud.

I had just stood to congratulate Charity on her culinary coup when Bristol burst from the dog gate and raced over to my side.

"Mom called and she's coming to pick me up—I'm sorry, but I have to leave early." Her voice cracked. "My uncle was in a wreck not far from us, just over that big hill. Black ice, they said. The other driver was killed. He's at the hospital. I have to..." Tears began coursing down her cheeks.

I placed a hand on her back. "Go," I said firmly. "I've got the dog room, no worries. I'm glad I was here so you didn't have to track me down. You watch for your mama, and I'll take over now." I pulled her into a hug.

When Bristol sat down on a barstool to wait for her mother, Kylie and Charity walked around to comfort her. I was pleased to see our Barks & Beans employees getting along so well, like a little family.

Bristol hadn't said how injured her uncle was, but I was sure it was serious if the other security truck driver had been killed. I would've thought an armored truck like that would survive a wreck pretty well, but it *was* a very steep hill with a sharp drop-off. It was basically the side of a mountain.

I'd moved into the dog petting area when Bristol's mom pulled up outside. I'd gotten to know Della Beth Goddard in a Bible study at church, and I'd been instantly impressed with her empathetic personality and soulful dark eyes. She was the kind of person who could pick up on how you were *really* feeling without having to guess. She folded her daughter into a hug, then they headed off to the hospital. There was a lot of love in Bristol's family, that much was evident.

Bo walked in the door and glanced my way. He walked straight over to ask if something had happened, so I filled him in. As we spoke, I absently watched the coffee bar, where a dark-haired woman was waiting on her drink at the counter. Her back was to me, but something about her drew my eye...

"Let's go visit them at the hospital tonight," Bo said. "Summer left me over half an apple pie—we could bring that to them."

"That's a great idea. I'd like to know how Bristol's uncle is faring." The small dog at my feet suddenly stood and started pacing, letting me know he had to be walked. I leashed him up, taking a final glance at the woman at the counter so I could figure out what seemed off about her.

She was already walking out the door, so again, I could only see her backside, but I realized what had pulled my attention to her. The woman's vibrant purple suede boots were covered in mud. Not just dried mud, either. They were wet partway up, like she'd been walking through snow. Or maybe she'd fallen into it, poor thing. Bless her heart. She was probably stopping in to warm up those wet feet. I hoped she'd get home soon to dry them off.

I took my leave from Bo, donning my coat and gloves before walking the dog out the side door. Bo had thoughtfully designed a fenced dog run that ran alongside the house.

The little dog's thin, wiry hair could hardly withstand the cold, so I tried to hurry him up with my repeated commands that he "go potty." He finally gathered up the courage to do so, leaving me a shockingly large mess to pick up. We kept plastic bags and a trash can outside for just such an occasion. I walked the shivering dog inside and unleashed him with his shelter friends before heading back out for cleanup duty.

I supposed some women would think I was going nowhere in life, owning half of a doggie cafe and occasionally doing pooper-scooper duty. But there was nothing more relaxing to me than hanging out with dogs. It had been that way since I was a kid. Starting around age six, I'd always had a dog—most often strays that I'd cleaned up and finally cajoled Auntie A into letting me keep. And although I'd had a lot of fun playing with Bo, I'd considered my dogs my best friends. Dogs were easier to talk to than girls my age, who'd seemed interested in things I wasn't. I'd shared some of my deepest philosophical ponderings with my mute dogs, who always seemed enrapt as I spoke.

Also, dogs were the only ones I could talk to about how my parents had died in a creek flood. Dogs didn't start crying, they didn't try to say things to make it better, and they didn't make awkward gestures to comfort me. Their very *presence* comforted me.

Not that Auntie A wasn't good at being there for me. She

told me stories of my parents' courtship and how they truly loved each other. She shared Mom's recipes and Dad's quirks, and she held me on those nights when I'd wake up crying.

But along the way, dogs had become a necessity to me. And now that I was surrounded by them, I'd discovered the job that made me feel I'd never have to work another day in my life.

I hoped Bristol's position at Barks & Beans would prove to be a good stepping-stone for her future career. From what I could see, she was already a hard worker. I hated that her day had been so traumatic, and I determined to do everything I could to lighten her load. Tonight, Bo and I would visit the hospital and get a better grip on what we could do to help the Goddard family.

3

I CALLED Bristol around suppertime to let her know we'd be dropping in with pie, and she seemed extremely grateful. She shared the unfortunate news that her uncle was in a coma and the doctors weren't certain how long it would last.

After fluffing Coal's pillow, refilling his food bowl, and turning on the TV for some background noise, I headed out to meet Bo in his truck around seven thirty. We talked on the way to the hospital.

"Crazy how things can change in a minute," I said. "I mean, we saw Clark just before his wreck, and he was right as rain. Now he's in a coma."

"It's awful," Bo agreed. His grip on the wheel was tight, and he drove a little slower than usual, probably watching for black ice. "It's weird, though. Clark grew up around here, and I've talked to the other driver before—Christian something or another. He was from Summers County. Those country boys would've *known* to slow down as they topped that hill."

I nodded, thoughtful. "You're right. Everyone around knows

the sunlight hardly hits that part of the road, thanks to those tall trees on both sides and the angle of that hill. We all watch out for that spot."

Bo pulled into the hospital. "It must've been a doozy of an accident, too. For Christian to be killed..." His voice trailed off as he got out and came around to open my door. Auntie A had made sure he learned the ways of a southern gentleman.

"I know." We fell silent as we walked into the quiet hospital. Bristol had told me where Clark's room was, so we took the elevator up. When we got out, we immediately caught sight of Bristol, her mom, and a teen guy I assumed was her brother, sitting on the couches at the end of the hallway.

Bristol looked like she'd dozed off, curled up at the end of the couch with a crocheted blanket draped over her legs. Her mom recognized me and stood.

"Macy," she said. "And this must be your brother, Bo?"

"Yes, he is. Bo, this is Della," I said by way of introduction. I stepped closer and gave her a hug. "I'm so sorry to hear of your brother."

As she pulled away, her eyes glistened with tears. "I know. We're all in shock. And Christian..." She cleared her throat, making an obvious effort to overcome her grief. "He was such a good man. It's unreal that he's gone."

The teen boy stood and slowly walked over to Bo. "Hi, I'm Ethan, Bristol's brother."

Bo smiled and clapped a friendly hand on his shoulder. "Nice to meet you."

Ethan turned to me. "Bristol's told me so much about your cafe and the dogs—it sounds like a blast."

It was obvious Ethan was in pain of some kind since he clutched at his side. I was about to tell him to come and visit Barks & Beans sometime, but I realized he probably rarely got out with his kidney disease. The fact that he was here tonight

for his uncle showed the depth of loyalty—or maybe gratitude—
he felt toward the man.

Bristol roused and blinked up at us. "Oh! Miss Hatfield,
Mr. Hatfield, I'm sorry—I was a little out of it there. Thanks so
much for coming."

As she stood, I held out the pie. "We came bearing gifts.
Our friend Summer—you know, her, Bristol, from the shelter?
—made this pie. Delicious as it was, we weren't able to polish it
off. It's all yours now."

Della took the pie and set it on the side table. "Thank you.
How thoughtful. I'll get some forks and plates from the nurses'
station." She headed down the hallway.

Bristol motioned for us to have a seat, so we each settled
into chairs. Ethan eased back onto the couch, moving like an
old man. My heart went out to the chronically ill teen. I didn't
know much about polycystic kidney disease, but the fact that
he was on regular dialysis told me how severe it was.

"We've been hearing bits and pieces about what happened,"
Bristol said, tugging at her green plaid shirt, which had ridden
up over her beltline. "The police came—a detective, actually. I
forget his name."

Ethan glanced up from the complex-looking word game
book he'd just cracked open. "It was Detective Charlie
Hatcher," he said.

Bristol nodded. "Yes, that's right. Anyway, the detective said
the security cameras got bashed up when the truck went over
the embankment, so they haven't been able to retrieve any
footage of the crash. It's clear the back doors were jarred open,
though. So the armored truck company—Stevens Security—is
checking to make sure all the money is intact."

Della returned, carrying paper plates and plastic utensils.
She began divvying up the pie.

I stopped her when she cut one piece really small. "Don't

give us any. We've already stuffed ourselves on pie the past couple of days. Cut some bigger pieces for the three of you."

"You're a sweetie," Della said, holding my eyes for a brief moment. I could tell with Della, those weren't idle words. She really thought I was a kind person, which was quite humbling. So often in life, people attributed bad or selfish motives to others. It was nice when someone seemed to peer into your heart and know that your only intent was to help.

Bristol leaned against her mom. "I was telling them about the wreck," she said. "Have you heard anything from Les Stevens? Was anything taken from the truck?"

"Les Stevens owns Stevens Security," Della explained as she handed her children pieces of pie. "And no, he hasn't called me yet, but he texted that he hopes to stop by tomorrow to see Clark."

"That's mighty nice of him," Ethan said, his voice full of sarcasm. "Now let's just hope the Stevens insurance plan will cover Uncle Clark's hospital care."

"Ethan!" His mom scolded. "Mr. Stevens has been nothing but kind through the years. He pays what he can afford to pay his employees."

Ethan spoke under his breath. "Meanwhile, he lives in a six-bedroom house, and he's single."

Bristol shot her brother a look. "*Anyway.* The doctors haven't said too much, except that they think Uncle Clark was knocked out on impact and slipped into a coma then."

"They said the driver's side was totally crushed." Ethan's incredulous look faded as he took another bite of pie. "This is delicious," he added.

Della cringed. "Let's not talk about the wreck anymore. And this pie *is* lovely. Thank you all so much for stopping in. How did things go at the cafe today? I heard you were busy?"

Conversation turned to lighter topics for a few moments,

but I could tell Della was anxious to check on Clark. I suggested she do that, and she let me follow her into his room. Monitors beeped steadily beside Clark's bed, and his eyes were closed as if he were asleep.

"I just can't believe it," she said, her voice wavering.

I squeezed her arm, wishing I could infuse her with fresh strength. "I know."

She turned to me. "There's no guarantee he'll ever come out of this coma. Then what will we do? I work hard, Macy, and so does Bristol, but it's just not enough to cover our mortgage and Ethan's health costs. Clark was such a blessing to us—he gave us so much I can never repay."

"That's what family is for," I said, my own emotions rising to the surface as I thought of how Bo had renovated the cafe, then offered me partnership in a ready-made business that was tailor-made for me. "I believe he knows you're there for him, Della. Be sure to talk to him when you're in here. You never know what he's picking up on."

She sniffled, releasing my hand to grab a tissue from the box on the bedside table. "You're right. I need to keep it together for the kids."

"Well, we should probably get back home and leave you all alone," I said. "I'll cover for Bristol tomorrow, and for as many days as she needs me to. We'll be praying Clark comes to quickly."

"Thank you," Della said, turning back to her unresponsive brother.

I walked out the door, struggling again to keep my own tears in check. If Bo were lying in that bed, I couldn't imagine what a disaster I'd be. Della was managing to keep a level head, probably for the sake of her children. I was sure that was taxing, trying to keep such strong emotions tamped down.

After saying goodbye to Bristol and Ethan, we gathered the empty pie plate and took the elevator to the main floor.

Bo broke the silence. "The least we could do is give Bristol a Christmas bonus. Could we give one to all our employees, so it doesn't look like we're singling her out?"

"Let's do it," I said. "I'll check the books, but I'm thinking we can afford it. Besides, it'll be that extra bit of goodwill and incentive in this first year of business."

"I'm proud of the business we've built, sis," Bo said.

I gulped and gave him a quick hug. "And I'm so proud of you."

Once I arrived home, I got online and stayed up late to wrap up my cybershopping by midnight. I managed to snag a great deal on a hunting knife I'd seen Bo eyeing on his phone, so I felt totally triumphant. Coal, who'd been walked for the last time and was obviously ready to go to bed, threw me more than one doleful stare until I finally gave in and closed my laptop.

"Let's get you upstairs. Go get on your pillow," I said.

He didn't really need the command. Once he saw me head for the stairs, he chugged right past me and thundered to his designated pillow bed. He kneaded the pillow three times exactly before dropping onto it like it was a cloud from heaven.

As I pulled on the lipstick tube-emblazoned pajamas Jake had given me on our second Christmas, I wondered if it was time to get rid of them. They always triggered a very visual memory of Jake and the way he'd suggestively handed me the perfectly wrapped present. "I got it at Macy's," he'd said, knowing I'd realize he'd bought it there because of my name.

I tried to blink back the memory, but it scrolled across my

mind anyway. Jake had been wearing his navy plaid PJ bottoms but no shirt, and his tousled blond hair had fallen over one of his beautiful hazel-green eyes. The Christmas tree lights were twinkling behind him, creating a halo effect.

I glanced down. The PJs fit me like a glove, and they were the comfiest cotton I'd ever worn. They washed like a dream and hadn't shrunk yet.

Nope, I wasn't going to trash these things just because they reminded me of Jake.

"He's not even worth thinking about," I said aloud.

Coal groaned from his curled-up position, not even opening his eyes.

"Good. I see you feel the same way." I tumbled into bed and sprawled out. That was something I hadn't been able to do when I was married to Jake, who tended to encroach on my space in his sleep.

But once I hit the light and tried to drift off, I couldn't get those flirtatious hazel eyes out of my mind. Of course, now I knew he'd used those eyes to charm several other women over the years. He'd truly believed I'd never find out. And I almost didn't, until he was forced to acknowledge the truth this past Christmas.

Still, it was weird not having another human in the large house to talk to. Sometimes, in the empty spaces, it was almost like my heart was beating too loudly, shouting for someone else to hear it.

I pulled the quilt over my head and sank into the darkness, but before I went to sleep, I recalled how Della had cringed when Ethan spoke of Christian's death. It was a cringe of grief, not just casual sadness. She was connected with Christian in some way. Something gave me the feeling she might've liked him.

I made a mental note to ask Bristol about it when she came back to work. If she had been romantically interested in Christian, Della Goddard had suffered a doubly traumatic day, and I doubted she'd soon recover from it.

4

COAL WOKE me with numerous wet-nosed nudges to my cheek, and I realized I'd hit snooze on my phone alarm three times. I threw on my only clean pair of jeans—an ill-fitting pair I'd shoved into the bottom of my drawer—and made a mental note to do laundry tonight. Adding a pale blue sweater and a long necklace, I considered my outfit complete. After doing a fast makeup job, I fed and walked Coal, then let him back in. I threw on my coat and boots and headed outside.

It was still below freezing, but the sidewalks had been heavily treated with salt, so it wasn't as slippery as it had been yesterday on my short walk to the cafe. Summer was just pulling up to the curb in the shelter van. I stopped as she parked. When she opened the door to let the dogs out, I noticed her long hair was tossed into a very messy bun. She looked as rumpled as I did.

I was more convinced than ever that we were kindred spirits. I didn't even attempt a cheery greeting, because I knew neither of us was feeling it this morning.

She handed me a couple of leashes and she took a couple. Our doggie crew this morning was adorable. One white Shih Tzu mix gazed up at me with little button-black eyes and I just wanted to drop everything and cuddle it.

Summer smiled. "I see you looking at him. Isn't he a doll? And he's very well-behaved. I figure he'll get adopted fast. But if you were interested..."

"Don't try to do a hard sale on me, Summer Adkins," I said. "I've already adopted one dog from you, and you could fit at least sixteen of this little lightweight into him. I have my hands full."

"I know you do." She gave her dogs' leashes a tug and walked them toward the cafe door, which was painted a glossy cherry red to match the white and red awnings. "I just know you'll talk him up for me."

"You got that right," I said, still fighting the nearly irresistible urge to pick up the tiny dog. The fuzzy pup was daintily clicking along the wooden flooring, going about half the pace of the larger dog leashed in my right hand.

We settled the shelter animals in the dog section, then Summer headed to the cafe to pick up her morning coffee. We'd added that as a perk—coffee on the house for whoever delivered the dogs every morning.

I knew what she'd order—a house coffee, black. I was impressed my friend knew how to savor the Costa Rican beans Bo had imported. Our house blend was intense, but it had citrus and brown sugar notes to it, so it felt both fresh and cozy. Bo knew far more about how the coffee beans were grown than I did, but he was always bragging that our house blend was grown at the highest altitude.

Summer chatted with Bo a moment at the coffee counter as I shuffled around with the dogs. Last month, she'd talked about asking Bo if he wanted to hang out sometime—aka have a date

—but she hadn't done it yet, and I wasn't really surprised. Summer didn't strike me as the kind of girl to make the first move. I determined to intervene soon and subtly urge Bo to ask her out. It was about time he put his money where his mouth was when he said he'd gotten over Tara.

By TEN IN THE MORNING, Barks & Beans was hopping. The doggie section stayed full of customers, which was great, since each visitor paid a cover charge of buying one drink. We gave the shelter a cut of that cover charge, so even if dogs didn't get adopted, we were helping out.

But today, dogs were going to be adopted. I'd already had two families claim the larger lab and shepherd mixes, and one woman had been sitting with the Shih Tzu mix for forty minutes solid. She seemed to be calling it "Binkie," so she was definitely getting attached.

An extremely tall, long-haired blond man strode into the cafe, exuding an air of foreignness. I edged closer to the rough wood and brick divider wall so I could get a better look. Sure enough, when he spoke, his voice was deep, with an unmistakable Germanic accent.

"A wreck has happened nearby?" he asked.

Milo peered at the oversized man through his thin glasses lenses. I happened to know he'd had laser surgery to correct his vision, so the glasses were entirely for show. He dressed the part of the deep but trendy barista to a T.

"Yes, there was a wreck yesterday." Milo's voice was hesitant.

"An armored truck, yes? The newspaper said one man died. Where is the other? He lived, yes?"

Milo turned his back on the man to pull his espresso shots. "He did."

The blond man turned, glancing over to the doggie section. His cold blue eyes lit on me for a split second. "And this man who lived, he had family perhaps?"

Okay, that was going way too far, like he was looking for Clark. Or maybe even Bristol?

I was about to walk over, tap the inquisitive punk on the shoulder, and tell him to back off, but Milo seemed to sense that he needed to be close-lipped. He shrugged, moving toward the mini fridge for the milk. The blond man fell silent and walked toward the pick-up end of the coffee bar.

He exchanged a few more words with Milo, but I couldn't pay attention to them because the woman who'd been cradling Binkie approached me. She'd decided to adopt him, so I told her how to get to the shelter so she could sign the paperwork.

When I glanced over again, the blond man was gone, so I assumed he'd left. I walked over to Milo and asked him for his take on the man.

"He gave me the chills." Milo pulled his cardigan sweater close. "Did you hear him? What did he want?"

"Sounded like he was probing around," I said.

"Well, I put him off. I played dumb and clammed up. But I did get a little information out of *him*—without even asking." Milo shot me a devious smile. "He had a room card on him for the Greenbrier. When he pulled cash from his pocket, the card fell out and I instantly recognized it."

Of course Milo did—his wealthy parents probably stayed at the posh resort all the time.

"Good work, Milo," I said. "You handled it well."

He grabbed a croissant from the fridge and popped it in the microwave. "I'm famished already," he said. "Charity stuffed these with chicken, pesto, and sun-dried tomatoes. I swear they're an entire meal. Try one—it's nearly lunchtime."

Milo had a tendency to come off like he was the boss around here. I usually tried to keep him in check and remind him he wasn't. However, he'd done a great job fielding the stranger's questions, so I let his imperious command slide. "Thanks. I'll get one a little later."

Milo took a big bite, then wiped pesto from his lips. "Oh, and one more thing. He had a gun in a shoulder holster under his jacket. I know it's nothing new, but with that guy, it seemed a little evil, you know?"

Milo was right—concealed guns were nothing new in southern West Virginia, and we had no rule against customers carrying in the cafe because we knew our clientele. But it did bother me that this man, who'd been asking invasive questions about the family of one of my employees, was wandering around town with a gun.

"Thanks for letting me know," I said. I headed back to the doggie section and promptly sent Bristol a text asking for Della's phone number. I told Bristol that I wanted to get updates on Clark's condition—which wasn't a total lie—but I also wanted to let her mom know there was a strange man in town who seemed to be looking for Clark.

DELLA RESPONDED PROMPTLY to my text. She said there'd been no change and Clark was still in the coma. She said it worried her that someone was looking for Clark, because Les Stevens had just called and told her that some of the cash had indeed been stolen from the truck—$500,000 worth, in fact. Because some money bags had been left in the truck, it had taken a while to determine how much had gone missing.

We agreed that it might be possible the Germanic guy had somehow gotten wind of the missing money and assumed Clark had stolen it. If you didn't know the entire situation, it would be logical to assume the surviving guard had stolen it. But we knew the full story—that Clark had been knocked into his coma on impact. On top of that, no one from around here would willingly drive a truck off that hill, knowing it could spell certain death.

After several moments, Della texted back that she'd called the police about the situation, and Detective Hatcher said the best they could do was alert the hospital staff on the floor to watch for the blond foreigner on the hall. The detective couldn't station officers outside Clark's room, because it was unclear when and if he would awaken from his coma.

I read the discouragement Della was writing between the lines and texted that I'd come over to the hospital tonight. Della said Bristol and Ethan were holding up alright, although Ethan hadn't been able to make it out to the hospital today.

When I got off the phone, I saw that Charity had arrived for the afternoon shift. During a lull, I motioned her over and asked if she had any extra chicken pesto croissants I could take to Bristol and her family tonight.

She gave a vigorous nod of her white head. "Oh, I'll have extras, hon. I'll be sure to leave some in the fridge in the back room. And take the rest of those mint macarons in that big white box, too. They're going to dry out." She leaned against the divider wall. "How's Bristol holding up? That poor child."

I loved how big Charity's heart was—the kindly widow would take in every lonely child in the world, if she could.

"Her mom says she's doing okay. Della's a great mom," I added.

"I'll just bet she is. I used to be a dental hygienist over at Doctor Belcher's office, and Della and her family were regulars for cleanings. Of course, she went by Della Beth back then, up until she got married. Law, but she had that thick, dark hair and dark eyes, and she was always so respectful with her 'yes ma'ams.' I hate that she's got so much on her plate. And I can't believe poor Clark is in a coma—though I have to tell you, he could be a bit of a rascal in the dentist's chair." She gave me a grin. "I think he's since straightened up considerably."

"It would seem so," I said. "He's done a lot to take care of Della and her family."

Bo, who'd been manning the coffee counter, motioned Charity back over since a short line was forming.

"Duty calls," Charity said. "Give Bristol a hug from me."

"Will do."

LATER THAT NIGHT, Della and Bristol were overjoyed to dip into the basket I'd prepared that included Charity's chicken croissants, the remaining macarons, and a carafe of hot house coffee.

"Thanks so much—the food here is...well, hospital food," Bristol said. "I'll take the rest of this back to Ethan. He loves Charity's cooking."

"How's he doing?" I asked.

A look passed between mother and daughter. Della spoke up. "To be honest, he's not so great today. His dialysis seemed to leave him a little dehydrated, so we're just trying to get more fluids into him and avoid a hospital visit."

I was about to offer to take him some Gatorade when a short, stocky man in chinos and a button-down shirt exited the elevator and made a beeline for Della. I reflexively moved closer to her side. Who was this man?

"Hi, Mr. Stevens," Della said, probably sensing my unease.

"Les, let me introduce you to Bristol's boss, Macy Hatfield—she and her brother own the Barks & Beans Cafe."

"Mr. Stevens," I said, shaking his outstretched hand. "It's nice to meet you. Your crew does good work."

The smaller man gave a cursory smile. "Don't they? And Clark Graham is one of the best." He turned to Della. "We're missing him this week. Christmas shopping season is in full swing, so we've had lots of pickups and deliveries. Is there any news?"

Della shook her head. "He's still unresponsive."

Les frowned, obviously upset, and took Della's elbow. "Could we talk?"

Without waiting for an answer, he steered her toward the couch. Bristol and I politely ambled off into the nearby snack room. We could still hear every word Les Stevens said, and given Bristol's silence, I knew she was eavesdropping just as hard as I was.

"It turns out, the money was bundled in stacks of fifty dollar bills, so we estimate it was only about twenty pounds' worth of cash," Les said.

There was a pause. "What're you saying, Les?" Della asked.

"Nothing, nothing," he said. "Just wondering if Clark had talked to you about this particular job before he went out on Friday."

"Why on earth would he do that?" Irritation was building in Della's voice. "Wait—Les, surely you don't think he and Christian *planned* this thing? You've got to be kidding me. Christian is *dead*, Les. There's no way he'd wreck a truck and risk both their lives in some stupid heist attempt."

"Please simmer down," Les said.

I imagined those words would make Della do just the opposite, and I was right.

"Simmer *down*? Les, you come in here—in the *hospital*, no

less—and you tell me to simmer down because you're practically accusing my brother of killing his partner and driving over a cliff for money? You don't know squat about my brother. He's the most honorable man you could ever hope to meet. He's earned every cent he's ever spent."

Zing. Bristol's eyes met mine, and I knew we were both inwardly cheering for her gutsy mom.

"I didn't know if maybe Christian—"

"Stop right there," Della said firmly. "Christian had no need for money. His parents run a huge restaurant chain and he always had money to burn."

"I guess you'd know," Les said. "You were dating him, right?"

"Good lands, Les, what are you, a detective? Yes, I'd gone out with Christian a few times. He was a kind man and Clark had nothing but good to say about him. I trust my brother's judgment."

"Of course, of course." Les seemed to be backtracking, trying to de-escalate things. "You know we'll make sure Clark is well taken care of," he continued. "Christian's family is having a closed casket funeral on Monday. Were you planning on going?"

Probably sensing a good opportunity to break in so the odious man wouldn't bother her mom, Bristol strode back to the waiting area and plopped down on a chair. I waited a couple of moments, then trailed out to join them.

Les stood up. "I suppose I won't stop by Clark's room, but please tell him I said we miss him if—I mean *when*—he wakes up."

He'd already dug the hole pretty deep, but that "if" had just sunk his ship.

Della's voice turned to ice. "I'll be sure to do that. Pardon me while I go check on my brother." She stood and whisked around Les.

"Okay." He gave us an awkward smile. "I'll stop back in again soon."

I wanted to say "Please, don't." Instead, I just waved him on. Once he was on the elevator, I sat down to talk with Bristol. "Are you going to be okay?" I asked. "That was pretty unsettling. He's very...aggressive."

Bristol's arms were wrapped tight around her middle and she shivered. "Yeah. I'm surprised he was that rude with Mom. I guess he really doesn't think Uncle Clark..." She teared up.

I reached over and patted her knee. "Don't let him get to you. I have a feeling your uncle's a fighter, just like the rest of your family."

Bristol smiled through her tears. "Thanks, Miss Hatfield. I'm hoping to be in to work on Monday."

"Don't rush yourself," I said, standing. "Please tell your mom I said goodbye. And try to get some rest, okay?"

The hospital was relatively quiet as I headed downstairs and out to my parking space. As I got into my car, I felt like I was being watched. I glanced around, but couldn't see much since darkness had already fallen. Just as my eyes started to adjust to the flickering parking lot lighting, I caught a movement in the driver's seat of a dark sedan. It looked like a larger-built man with long hair. Squinting to see him better, it was clear his hair was light-colored. In fact, from what I could make out, he looked a lot like the Germanic interrogator from the cafe.

I started the car and slowly pulled out of my parking space. Plucking up courage, I drove directly past the sedan—which turned out to a Hyundai—on my way out. It seemed the driver's seat had somehow been vacated...or else the big man was hunkering down on the floor of the car.

There was no way I was going to pull to a stop to get out and check. Instead, I phoned Detective Hatcher—who I happened to have as a contact in my phone list—and let him know I was pretty sure I'd spotted the blond man sitting in a dark Hyundai sedan in the hospital parking lot. He assured me he'd have someone swing by and check on it, which was comforting, because I didn't want to have to alert Della. Her evening had already been distressing enough.

5

Sᴜɴᴅᴀʏ sᴇᴇᴍᴇᴅ like it was going to be a relaxing day. Bo and I went to our church—the same one we'd grown up in—and I sang in the choir. There was something about standing up there, looking out over the group of kind-hearted neighbors who made up the congregation, that never failed to lift my spirits. I was one of a chatty group of sopranos, and we got along famously. I missed seeing Della and her family in their usual pew, but I knew she'd been running around with hospital visits and long work hours.

Unfortunately, during the sermon, my mind started wandering. Why had Les Stevens been so hard on Della? It seemed he was hitting her while she was down, insinuating that her brother was crooked. And if it *was* the creepy blond man in the car last night, why did it feel like he was skulking around, watching Bristol and her family? Maybe Clark knew too much, and the man was watching for a chance to pull the plug on him, like in the movies? I checked my phone, hoping for a text from Detective Hatcher, but there was none. I was guessing the blond man had evacuated the parking lot right after I left.

The fact remained that someone must've stolen half a million in cash from the crashed armored truck, and the cops were having no luck finding it. The blond man had to be integral to everything that was going on, but how? Had he stolen the money and Clark could identify him, or was he only *looking* for the money, hoping to get more information out of Clark?

Bo nudged me at the end of the service. "Did you catch any of that? Usually you're taking frantic notes." His sky blue eyes flickered over my face, concerned.

"I'm fine," I said. "Just having trouble concentrating today."

"You might be hungry," he said. "You want to hit that fusion restaurant after you walk Coal?"

My needs were probably as simple as my dog's—for a cozy shelter, regular food and drink, loyal company, and a nice head rub from time to time. Sadly, Jake had never been good at head rubs, and his loyalty was nonexistent.

Thankfully, my brother was always there for me, and he knew me well. "Sounds great," I said. Maybe food would help me focus, and Bo would probably have some insight as to why the blond man was lurking around. After all, my brother hadn't just been the coffee company vice president all those years in California—he'd recently revealed that Coffee Mass had been a front for his undercover job with the DEA. This year, he'd taken early retirement from both positions before launching Barks & Beans, but I had a feeling Bo could sniff out illegal shenanigans far better than I could.

That didn't mean I would stop trying to get to the bottom of things, for Bristol's sake. Someone had to.

On Monday morning, I was able to take my day off because Bristol felt she could come back to work. I had just settled in with my second cup of Irish breakfast tea and a boiled egg-on-toast sandwich when my doorbell rang. Coal jumped to attention, skidding along the wood floor until he body-slammed into the back door.

Thankfully, I'd taken time to throw on jeans and a sweater. Usually on my days off, I stayed in PJs as long as possible. I stood and walked over by Coal, ordering him to hush up. I might as well have ordered a loaded coal train to stop on a dime, because once he started barking, there was no quieting him.

I cracked the door. A shorter man stood outside, wearing dress pants and a crisp shirt and tie. Perhaps he was a Jehovah's Witness?

He gave a tentative smile, glancing down as if nervous that the humongous dog he'd heard barking was likely to emerge. "Hi, are you Macy Hatfield? The lady at the cafe counter sent me over here. I needed to talk with a manager?"

Bo didn't head into work until afternoon, so I supposed I was the manager on duty. "Yes, I'm Macy," I said. "And you are?"

"Joe Watkins," he said. "I'm with Stevens Security. We're following up on any suspicious activity that might've occurred after our security truck crashed, not far from here. I'm sure you heard about the wreck?"

"Bad news travels fast," I said, pushing against Coal. The dog was leaning against me so hard, he was liable to shove me right out the door.

"Right. Well, I wondered if anyone unusual visited the cafe on Friday, sometime after three in the afternoon? By unusual, I mean they were carrying a large bag or their coat seemed bulky, that kind of thing."

Did he really think someone had climbed down a steep hill,

loaded up with 500 grand in cash, then stopped by the cafe on their way home? I supposed it wasn't outside the realm of possibility—it had been a cold, icy day, after all—but it seemed highly unlikely.

"Let's see...Kylie and Charity were there at that time, as were my brother and I," I said. "I can talk to them and ask if they saw anyone. As for me...hm." I tried to recall how things had played out that afternoon. "It was Black Friday, so the cafe was busy. Lots of moms were coming and going, carrying shopping bags, but that was nothing unusual. Oh—there was one thing that caught my attention. A woman with black hair had really wet, muddy purple suede boots. I didn't catch a glimpse of her face, though. I guessed that she'd fallen on the ice at some point and gotten her boots slushy."

I figured Joe would be disappointed by my lack of information, but instead, he looked like I'd piqued his interest. "She could be significant," he said. "See, we found out it was a woman who'd placed a call to emergency services about our wrecked vehicle. She made that call from one of the only payphones in town—the one right at the corner of your block. Maybe she decided to come inside and warm up."

"But how would she carry all that money?" I closed my eyes, trying to envision her. "As I recall, she wasn't carrying any shopping bags."

"With fifty dollar bills, you'd be surprised how much you could fit in a normal-sized purse," he said, his voice thoughtful. "Or even boots."

I supposed he had a point there, though I couldn't imagine why she would've come inside with loot in her boots or purse. Then again, Mr. Stevens had told Della it was only twenty pounds of cash, so maybe she'd tucked it away and assumed no one would notice. "I'll ask around and keep my eye out for her," I said.

"Thanks." He nodded and turned, walking down the steps and out my back gate. He must've parked elsewhere since he kept walking once he hit the sidewalk.

I shut the door and Coal finally backed up a little, his amber eyes questioning . "Yeah, he was okay. Thanks for giving me so much space," I said sarcastically.

It wasn't until I sat back down with my warmed-up sandwich that I realized Joe Watkins hadn't offered me a card or given me the number where I could reach him. I supposed I'd have to call Stevens Security directly if I discovered anything.

I had a feeling I'd seen the black-haired woman somewhere before, but I didn't know where. Maybe she was a regular customer. She was just average height, and nothing about her stood out as unusual except her boots, which she'd doubtless since cleaned or even gotten rid of, if they'd been ruined by the snow. Suede wasn't the most forgiving material in winter.

I took my final sip of tea and rubbed behind Coal's tall ears. Those clipped ears weren't as mobile as many Danes' floppy, unclipped ears, but Coal managed to flatten them back toward his head every time I rubbed them. He threw a large paw onto my lap and leaned into me.

"You're just a big baby, aren't you?" I crooned.

My cell phone buzzed, so I snatched it from the side table. Bristol's despondent voice sounded on the other end.

"Hi, Macy. I'm sorry to bother you. Listen, my mom is sitting with a lady right now, so she can't come home, but my brother is having a hard day. Would it be okay if I headed home after lunch?"

"Of course." I deliberately hadn't planned anything today, figuring Bristol might have an emergency arise.

"I'm so sorry. I'm hoping I'll be around tomorrow since Mom will be home for Ethan. He's just really discouraged with everything with Uncle Clark, plus he's due for dialysis tomorrow and he's really feeling it. It's too bad he's not well enough to get out a little—he'd love to see all the dogs here."

I had a brainstorm. "Maybe he can't come to the dogs, but how about I bring a dog to him? Bo and I would be glad to drop by tonight with my dog, if you think Ethan would be up to it."

"Oh my word—Coal? He'd love Coal! Sure. That'll give him something to look forward to. Thank you!"

"And count on us to bring you some supper, too," I added. Aunt Athaleen always said church people should "put their money where their mouth is" and bring food when people were feeling poorly, not just show up at the hospital hoping for some kind of grand reception. Although I wasn't the best cook in the world, I totally agreed with her, and I knew Bo could come up with some delicious dish he'd be happy to prepare for the Goddards.

"Thank you so much, Miss Hatfield. I'll plan to head home around 12:30."

"I'll be over at the cafe by then."

After hanging up, I puttered around, cleaning up my breakfast dishes. Coal trailed after me, probably hoping for a treat. I grabbed one and tossed it to him, which he barely chewed before swallowing. "Sorry, boy, but I'm going to have to head into work today after all."

He gave me one of those semi-yowls that made it seem like he wanted to have a conversation. "I know, I know," I said. "I'd hoped to hang out with you today, too. But tonight we'll do something fun."

Looking hopeful, Coal trotted back to his pillow and gnawed on his favorite bone. I hoped my gigantic dog would behave himself tonight at the Goddards'. I'd use his dog harness so I could restrain him quickly, if need be. But I suspected Coal would be just what the doctor ordered for Ethan.

Sᴜʀᴇ ᴇɴᴏᴜɢʜ, Bo was happy to whip up a batch of Auntie A's cheesy bacon potato soup, and when I got home from work, I fixed a fresh salad and muffins. Bo brought his truck over at seven, and I handed him the food before loading Coal into the back of the truck. I sat down next to him on the wheel well, gripping his harness tightly. Bo drove slowly through town so as not to jolt us. Coal tipped his head toward the sky, his tongue lolling out to catch the fresh breeze, but he stayed pressed against my legs for the duration of the short trip.

The Goddards lived up a side street in an adorable dark gray Cape Cod. Bo helped us out of the back, then he grabbed the food while I rang the bell. Bristol was quick to answer the door, and a smile stretched across her face when she saw Coal. She gave a little clap. "He's going to be so thrilled. Come this way."

She led us into the kitchen so Bo could set the food on a counter. "Mom just got home—she said she had a long day. She was so thankful you all were bringing food. And man, does it smell delicious." She motioned us down the hallway toward an open door on the left. "Y'all can go right in—Ethan's expecting you. I'll tell Mom you're here."

Bo went in first, and Coal and I pulled up the rear. The room was small and decorated in a nautical theme. Ethan sat on his twin bed, his eyes widening when Coal stepped close to him. The dog seemed to take up most of the room.

"Sorry I can't get up right now," Ethan said.

"No need to apologize." I tugged at Coal's harness so he'd back up a little. "Sit."

Coal surprised me by actually following instructions. He gently nudged Ethan's hand with his wet nose. It was like he sensed the teen wasn't feeling well.

"This is Coal, and as you can see, he's pretty friendly. I think he likes you already."

Ethan beamed. "I'm so jealous of Bristol, working with dogs all the time. Dogs are my jam, you know?"

"Dogs and ships?" I asked, glancing around at the pictures of warships on his walls.

"Yeah. I used to want to go into the Navy," he said. "That's never going to happen, but I do hold the number three rank worldwide in my battleship video game, so there's that." He gingerly stretched his long fingers in front of Coal's nose, and the dog licked them.

"I can see you're a dog person," I said. "Coal can usually tell if someone's scared around him, which makes him nervous. But you're not."

"He's dying to visit your cafe," Della said, leaning on the doorframe. Her long hair draped over her shoulders, and it seemed to engulf her slight frame. I was fairly certain she'd lost weight over the past few days. "Maybe we can bring him by later this week."

"Or we could pick him up," I offered.

"You're too kind," Della said. "We appreciate you two so much. You've brightened things up in this dark time."

"We should get going," Bo said, probably sensing, as I did, that Della was tired and needed to eat.

Ethan was busy petting Coal, who had sat down in front of him. "How's Clark doing?" I asked.

"No changes," Della said, turning aside to swipe at a rogue tear.

I held off a moment before asking, "Do you happen to know a guy named Joe Watkins who works for Les Stevens? He stopped by asking questions about the wreck, and I forgot to get his number."

"Joe Watkins, you say? I've never heard of anyone by that name at the company. What did he say his job was?"

I thought back. "He didn't really say. He just told me he was following up on things."

Della gave me an uneasy look. "I could swear there's no one by that name there. It's a small operation."

"Uh-oh," Bo said. "Not good, sis."

My stomach sank. "Could you give me Mr. Stevens' number?"

Della recited the number so I could plug it into my phone. Afterward, I turned back to Coal, who was now lying on the floor, getting a belly rub from Ethan.

"C'mon, boy," I wheedled, knowing Coal was having the time of his life. "We need to let everyone eat their supper while it's hot."

I gave Coal's leash a gentle tug, and he reluctantly rose to his feet. "He's had a great time with you, Ethan," I said. "You're welcome to visit him anytime you feel like it. My door's always open."

Ethan smiled, his brown eyes sparkling. "You've got a deal, Miss Hatfield. Bye, Coal."

I followed Bo and Della down the hallway, with Coal trudging behind. Bristol was in the living room, eating on the couch. She waved. "Sorry I didn't talk more, but I was starving and this soup smelled *so* good. I love that bacon in it."

Bo nodded. "Gives it that extra kick, doesn't it?"

"It was good to see you all," I added, as Della ladled out a couple of bowls. "And let me know if that Joe guy stops by here. In the meantime, I'm going to ask Les about him."

6

THE MINUTE COAL and I got into the house, I gave Les Stevens a call and asked if Joe Watkins worked for Stevens Security.

"Joe who?" he asked, his voice irritated. His TV blared in the background.

"Joe *Watkins*," I said loudly.

The TV quieted, as if he'd turned it down. His voice was sharp. "No, I've never in my life met a Joe Watkins. What's this all about?"

I explained how a man claiming to be Joe had come around, saying he was with Stevens Security.

"And he was following up on the wreck, he said?" Les groaned. "Why'd you tell him anything?"

Now I was getting irritable. "I assumed he was telling the truth. Why else would he want to know who'd come into the cafe that day?"

"What'd he look like?" Les asked abruptly.

"Uh, well—let's see. Dressed nice with a tie and dress pants. Kind of on the shorter side with black hair and a tan—"

"Okay, thanks for letting me know." Les abruptly hung up.

I stared at the phone. "You've *got* to be kidding me. I take the time to call you about a fake employee, and you hang up on me?"

I called Bo next, running Les' weird behavior past him, since he was already aware that Joe Watkins had pulled the wool over my eyes.

"What do you think is going on?" I asked. "First of all, I don't get why someone would come in, pretend to be with Stevens Security, only to ask about unusual people who stopped in after the wreck."

Bo's deep voice filled the line. "I'd wager that 'Joe' believes someone made off with the $500,000, and he's trying to get to that person before the cops do. Before we try to figure out Les' reaction, what exactly did you *tell* Joe Watkins?"

"Nothing solid. I just recalled some black-haired woman coming in on Black Friday with wet purple suede boots, that's all. I told him she wasn't even carrying shopping bags, and I didn't get a look at her face. Although she did seem familiar somehow. Still, that was hardly anything for him to go on. What's he going to do, go door-to-door and ask women if they own purple boots?"

"Exactly. Nah, he won't be able to do anything with that information. Did he tell *you* anything helpful?"

I thought back. "Well, he did say that it was a woman who'd called emergency services—from a pay phone in town. How would some random dude know that information?"

"Good question. Ouch!" Bo gave a short yelp. "Sorry, Stormy just decided to claw up my shoulder like some maniac mountain climber. Hang on a sec while I extract her." He took a moment, then heaved a new parent kind of sigh as he picked up the phone. "Anyway, back to Joe—I'm guessing he has some connections."

"With cops? Or maybe Les?" That seemed to fit. My words tumbled out as I tried to make sense of things. "Maybe that's why Les hung up so fast, because his conning spy guy was off the books? Maybe...maybe Les is trying to find the money for himself?"

"I don't think so. If he's looking for the money, he wouldn't have to be sneaky about it, because he must be hoping to restore it to the owner. Think about it—$500,000 goes missing with Stevens Security—who's going to want to hire them to move their money or valuables after that? It's a blow to his company if that money isn't found, and found quickly."

Bo did have a good point. "Then why was Les so abrupt?" I pressed.

"You've told me he tends to act like a jerk to Della, right? Maybe he's just a rude type of guy with no social graces."

I sighed. "You're an awfully insightful dude, you know that? I don't care what Auntie A did say about you."

He laughed. "And I won't tell you what she said about *you*, sis."

It felt good to joke with my brother, knowing he was just a few doors down instead of all the way across the country. "So...should we let Detective Hatcher know about Joe?"

"Yes. You should call him, give him the details of what he said to you and what he looked like. That way they can keep an eye out for him in case he shows up somewhere else asking questions."

"Gotcha," I said. "I'll call now. Thanks, Bo."

"Anytime."

I FELT like the town weirdo who was always calling or texting Detective Hatcher at night, but I trusted Bo's advice. Plus, I had to believe the man didn't hate me, since he'd actually given Bo and me his personal cell number. I think he respected that Bo had been in the DEA, so by extension, he respected me.

Also, I *had* helped expose a murdering criminal just a month and a half ago, so there was that.

Sure enough, Charlie Hatcher seemed happy to hear from me. Unlike a stereotypical detective, the fifty-something married man wasn't particularly foreboding—although I knew he could be intimidating if he wanted to be.

As he asked why I was calling, I could easily picture him. He had a dimple in his cheek and kind hazel eyes that made people want to talk to him, but his steely gray hair and the set of his chin told the real story—that he would doggedly stick to his cases until he solved them. He was an asset to the town, that much was certain.

I told him about my conversation with the fake Joe Watkins. When he asked a few questions to clarify things, I was sure he was taking notes. I also shared I'd asked Les Stevens about Joe, and he'd categorically denied that a man by that name even worked for him.

"By the way, did you ever find that tall blond man in the dark Hyundai?" I asked, trying to shift out of the way as Coal decided to climb onto the couch next to me. He took up two entire seats' worth of space.

"No. Unfortunately, he wasn't in the parking lot by the time I got a unit over there." I could hear his pen tapping at the table. "Miss Hatfield, while I can assure you that we'll be looking into this, I'll also let you know that we're exploring other angles in this truck heist case."

"Oh, okay. Of course," I said awkwardly. "Sorry to bother you so late."

"No, no—it's never a bother. You've been extremely helpful. Tell your brother I said hi."

I GOT out of the tub, only to find Coal frolicking around my room with his bone. He seemed to have gotten a fresh dose of energy, which I put down to his excitement over his visit with Ethan. Coal seemed to be an extrovert dog, even though most dogs probably were. I made a mental note to walk him through town more often so he could see people, although this time of year, walks were a bit iffy.

Maybe he needed to spend more time with Bo's frisky kitten. However, I had a feeling that even a huge dog like Coal couldn't tame that little whirlwind.

As I cozied into my freshly-washed sheets, I wondered what Detective Hatcher had meant when he said they were following up on other angles. What other angles were there? There didn't seem to be a lot of suspects in this heist case.

Maybe the money had just spilled out of the truck as it bounced to the forest floor? But the police would've definitely found that when they were examining the wreck scene.

Unless one of the cops was dirty?

Probably not. Lately I'd been binge-watching old episodes of *Poirot*, so I was probably seeing underlying motives everywhere. I'd learned to suspect the unsuspected.

Maybe in real life the most obvious solution was correct. And if I were Detective Hatcher, the people at the top of my suspect list would be the banker who'd passed the money to the truck drivers and the truck drivers themselves.

As for the drivers, I couldn't see Christian or Clark risking their lives by driving off a cliff when they could simply disable the cameras, concoct a story of a robber, then find a clever way to hide the money. And if Clark *had* somehow managed to rob the truck before falling into a coma, why didn't he take all of the money? Why leave any behind?

And I didn't know who the banker was, but I had to assume Detective Hatcher was all over it. Sure, I could swing by the bank, but there was no casual way to ask who handed the money off to the armored truck drivers on Black Friday.

I pulled my eye mask down, hoping to block out the moonlight that flooded through my curtains. I supposed it would be wisest if I'd trust that the police had matters safely in hand, now that Detective Hatcher had every bit as much information as I did about the wreck—and more.

Coal gave a slight whine from his pillow that told me he was already falling asleep. It was time for me to put the case of the inexplicable heist out of my mind and go to sleep. Besides, I had plenty to think about, like planning a raffle giveaway for the upcoming Girl's Day Out shopping event in town. I needed to discuss marketing ideas with Bo, our staff, and with Summer. Once I resolved to start focusing on my job at Barks & Beans, I was able to roll over and doze off without a care in the world.

7

I WAS glad it was my day in the doggie cafe, so Bristol was able to accompany Ethan for his dialysis. From what I understood, Della was putting in long hours as a caregiver, sitting with an Alzheimer's patient, so she couldn't go along with her son.

It occurred to me that, although Auntie A's death this past January from cancer had seemed to come with almost no warning, we had been spared watching her mind deteriorate in front of us. I knew dementia brought a special kind of heartache, and I was thankful there were people like Della in the world, who allowed patients to stay in their own homes as long as possible.

Kylie had the coffee machines humming, and Summer was already setting up the dogs in the Barks section when I arrived. Bo had the day off, although he probably wasn't sleeping in. My brother was a runner, so quite often he'd be out in the early morning or even late night, pounding the pavement.

Jimmy, our high school bus driver-turned-barista, was busy straightening chairs. He had such a bulky build, he kept bumping chairs out of place even as he scooted others in. I found it endearing that his large, intimidating frame also hid a large heart. Jimmy was always the first to fill in for me with the dogs whenever I needed a reprieve. Not only was he good with animals, but he seemed to get a fast and accurate read on people, which I appreciated.

"How's Jenny?" I asked. Jimmy always loved to talk about his wife, whose name wasn't hard to remember. Jimmy and Jenny Arbogast.

"Doing okay. I dug her a new flowerbed this weekend, and she's been circling things in her flower catalogue ever since. I believe this is going to cost me a small fortune, Miss Macy."

I laughed. "Tell her I split some iris bulbs last month and I'm happy to give her a bunch. They're some of Auntie A's prize-winners."

Summer whipped her head around. "Are you talking about those deep purple ones? Could I have a few, too?"

I nodded. "The deep purple, the peach, and that orange and white frothy one that always reminds me of a Dreamsicle."

Summer was practically salivating. "Now, you know how I love flowers, Macy Hatfield. Next time you split bulbs, you'd better offer some to *all* your friends."

I shrugged. "I didn't think you had room in your flowerbeds for more."

She unleashed a sleek brown dog with floppy ears. "Trust me, I'll *make* room for your Auntie A's flowers."

Since the ground was likely too hard to plant, I promised Jimmy and Summer that I'd deliver the iris bulbs in time for planting this spring. Grabbing a house coffee, I headed into the doggie section and let Summer give me the rundown on each canine.

By the time she left, the cafe was opening. I observed each of the four shelter dogs, trying to imagine what kind of owners they'd need. The floppy-eared brown one seemed older and very low-key. Summer had said he wasn't great with kids, so he'd likely need to be matched with an older couple or a single person. There were two mid-sized, spotted dogs that frisked around with each other—they seemed like tight friends. No one had adopted two dogs at a time...yet. But there was always a first time.

Finally, there was a smaller sized dog that looked like a pit bull mix. She shot nervous glances up at me—no surprise, given Summer's story that she'd been dropped in a dumpster. She certainly wasn't aggressive, but I knew abandoned dogs had their own issues. She'd need someone who knew her background and had the patience to work with her through her inevitable phobias.

The customers of Barks & Beans were always a mixed bag. Some would take time to open the divider gate and visit with the dogs, while others seemed to enjoy observing at a distance. Some were truly interested in adopting, while others just wanted to unwind with a dog on their lunch break. I tried to catch the eye of anyone who came in the door, hoping they'd feel pulled to the Barks section.

Which was why I noticed the blond Germanic man the moment he came into the cafe. He didn't notice me, though. Instead, he walked straight to the coffee counter and struck up a conversation with Kylie. Seeing him again in the daylight, I was positive he was the man I'd seen parked outside the hospital.

The brown dog was sitting sedately with an older woman, and the younger dogs were playing with a rope toy in the corner, so I edged closer to the brick and wood divider wall. I had to step around the pit bull mix, who was dozing on a pillow.

Unless I missed my guess, the man seemed to be flirting with Kylie. He was pointing to her tattoo, then motioning to his own arm—maybe he had a tattoo as well? Hopefully he wasn't motioning to his concealed firearm, which he was likely carrying. But Kylie smiled back, so he couldn't be annoying or threatening her. Jimmy wasn't behind the counter, so I assumed he was doing something in the back room.

I inched closer and leaned against the wall like I was tired. As Kylie bustled around to prepare the man's coffee, I caught one of his questions.

"Did you know the family of the man who died in the wreck?" he asked, his voice dripping with false sympathy.

I sadly hadn't briefed Kylie about watching for the nosy man, so she readily answered him. "No, but I know the niece of the man who's in a coma," she said. "She actually works here."

He was turned away from me, but I could practically *feel* his anticipation as he asked the next question.

"And this girl, is she working today?" He turned to scan the cafe.

He certainly got an eyeful, because I was striding straight toward him, just as fast as my five foot three-sized legs could carry me along.

Kylie froze in place with the man's coffee drink, her face registering instant concern. It was probably obvious I was on the warpath.

"She's not working today, but I am," I said, my voice far from measured. "And I'm the manager here. I'd suggest you don't come into *my cafe* asking questions about *my employee* again."

I was face to chest with the tall man, who towered over me. He cracked a hesitant smile.

"Perhaps I do not understand the ways of your country," he said. "I am staying nearby, and all the staff are talking about this armored truck crash. It has raised my interest as well."

I was about to raise *his* interest in buzzing off from Barks & Beans for good. "I understand," I said, offering that honeyed smile of the South that meant you had another thing coming. "But if you continue to ask personal questions of my employees, I'll be forced to report you to the local authorities—the police," I said clearly.

As I expected, the word "police" seemed to translate well to any language, and the man started to apologize.

"Of course, I will ask no more questions of you. Perhaps I must find another place for my morning coffee," he said.

"Perhaps you should." My posture and my voice were unyielding. I knew it was bad business, but I didn't care.

He offered me a final, conciliatory smile, which I did not return, then took the coffee he'd paid for and strode out.

Kylie gave a slow clap. "Holy smokes, Batman. You've got some steel in your spine."

Jimmy strode out of the back room, cradling two stacks of small plates in his large arms. "You wouldn't believe how hard I had to look for these." He seemed to realize I was standing in the Beans section, no doubt looking a bit hostile. "What's going on?" he asked. "Did I miss something?"

ONCE THINGS HAD CALMED down a little, I texted Detective Hatcher to fill him in on the Germanic man's persistent questioning about the Goddard family. While he couldn't exactly pull the man in for asking questions in a cafe, he did assure me he'd send the patrol out to the hospital to check on Clark Graham.

I considered calling Bristol, but I doubted the blond man would be able to find her at the dialysis center. She didn't need the extra worry right now.

Bo texted around four, asking if I wanted to drop by his place once I closed the cafe at five. He'd have supper waiting, then he wanted me to accompany him to my first town council meeting.

"We need to keep abreast of changes in town," he said. "Plus, two are stronger than one when we represent Barks & Beans."

I agreed, sensing that my brother wanted me by his side tonight for some reason. Once I'd closed up, I went home, walked and fed Coal, grabbed my tube of watermelon-colored lip gloss, then headed over to Bo's place. His bungalow-style house was only a few houses down from me, and it was very different from Auntie A's big Colonial. He'd decorated the inside like a beach house—all light colors and plants and wicker furniture.

Stormy the kitten ran straight at me when I came in the unlocked door, swiping at my feet so I could hardly walk. "Quite an attack cat you're raising there," I shouted into the empty living room, assuming Bo was in his room. I picked up the writhing kitten and tried to get her to calm down, but whispering didn't seem to have the same effect it did on jittery dogs. Instead, she must've thought I was hissing at her, because she raised her little multicolored paw and fearlessly booped my nose. I couldn't even pretend to be a cat person.

Bo came out of his room, wearing a clean white tee. It was obvious that he'd continued working out, even though he was no longer a Marine or in the DEA. My brother was the type of guy who liked to be prepared, and he wanted to be tougher than anyone else in the room. He'd always been that way—and he'd always had a crew of guys who'd followed him around, sensing his leadership. I wondered if he missed that here, but I supposed he was still leading the Barks & Beans crew, albeit not out on dangerous missions.

"I fixed us some hot subs—let me get them out of the oven,"

he said. "Can you grab the banana peppers and toppings from the fridge?"

"You got it. Thanks."

As we sat down with our plates, I told Bo about the weirdo blond man who'd been asking about Bristol.

"Why didn't you call me first?" he demanded. "That guy could've done anything, and you don't have a weapon."

I took a hefty bite of sub. "I'm sure Jimmy would've come out if there was a ruckus."

"You said he didn't even hear what was going on, and anyway, if that guy's packing heat, he's still got the drop on you."

I laughed. "You know you're talking like a gumshoe detective from the twenties."

His freckled face remained impassive, even as Stormy was clawing her way up into his lap. "I'm serious. Macy, call me first."

"Will do," I promised. Bo wouldn't waste a second if I ever *did* have to call him to the cafe for backup. "Now let's finish this fine meal so we can go to that council meeting and catch up on all the latest."

THE CITY HALL chairs were plush, so I was nearly dozing off as the minutes were read. Most of the town business was uninteresting and had little effect on our business, but when they started discussing the Girl's Day Out, I perked up. It seemed many store owners were giving away free food that day, so my mind started whirling around possibilities for small baked items we could offer, or maybe hot coffee drinks.

When the floor was opened for comments, a woman strode

past my chair. Her shoes were in my line of sight, and I sat up straighter the moment I saw them.

She was wearing purple suede boots. They'd been wiped down, but they were definitely the exact same pair she'd been wearing in Barks & Beans the day the armored truck had crashed.

8

The black-haired woman stood at the microphone, adjusting it. Now that she was facing me, I realized she was Sheldia Powers, the librarian who'd donated discarded books so Bo could stock the shelves at Barks & Beans. At the time, I'd felt the single woman's generosity stemmed from hopes of snagging Bo's attention. Given the way she was now throwing nervous glances at my brother, I knew my guess had been right.

She introduced herself as the Bookmobile director at the library and launched into a report.

"As I've mentioned before, the Bookmobile bus has been in dire need of repairs—so many of them, in fact, that we haven't been able to afford to get it running." Her pale face looked even more blanched under the cold overhead lights. She was pretty in a somewhat ethereal way. Her untamed cloud of black hair seemed to frame her face, and her blue eyes and red lips gave her a certain Snow White flair.

Those lips cracked into a smile. "I'm happy to report that an anonymous donor has given us enough money to buy a brand new bus." A bit of hectic color came into her cheeks as she warmed to her topic. "Plus, the donation was large enough to set aside money to prepare the 'go bag' backpacks for our foster care children in town. These packs will include new, award-winning books, along with necessities the children can take to their new placements, so they won't be empty-handed when they are placed with new families." She gave a little clap, unable to control her joy.

The audience followed her lead and broke into a round of brief applause. It was heartening that someone in town was using their money to support reading efforts—and more importantly, foster children, whose number had exploded in our area.

As Sheldia walked past us to take her seat, she caught Bo's eye and offered a little wave. In his favor, my brother did give a nod and a brief wave of his own. Although he was oblivious to most interested advances, he had still been raised to be polite.

When the council released, a wiry, grizzled man made a beeline for us. He shook Bo's hand.

Bo introduced me. "This is Chevy Whitfield—he's the man who built Barks & Beans for us." The man's name was pronounced like a Chevy truck.

I shook the man's hand. "So pleased to meet you. You've done great work."

As the men fell into a conversation, I wandered toward the back of the room, where Sheldia was making her way to the door. She turned as I got close, offering me a brief smile. "You must be Macy? I went to school with your brother."

I'd forgotten that, but it made sense. Sheldia might've had the hots for Bo a good many years now.

"Thanks for the books you donated to our cafe," I said, following her outside. "You're like one of those old-fashioned

Appalachian pack-horse librarians, delivering books to the needy."

I'd definitely gotten her attention, since she stopped short on the sidewalk. "I guess so. I have a real burden for literacy, I guess. Books were some of my best friends growing up."

I nodded, falling into step beside her until she slowed by a beat-up white minivan. The librarian certainly wasn't living large—and I was surprised she had a minivan.

"Do you have kids?" I blurted out, only to wish I hadn't spoken so hastily.

She followed my gaze to her van and chuckled. "Oh, no. I just bought this van to transport boxes of books. Although I am currently in the process of becoming an approved foster parent, so come to think of it, the van'll come in handy."

She had her keys in hand and was about to step onto the street to get in the vehicle. But I had one more question to ask. I placed a hand on her arm.

"Say, have you dropped into Barks & Beans yet? I think you'd enjoy it, and you could see how nice your books look on our shelves."

I wondered if she'd answer me honestly or if she'd try to hide her visit to the cafe on Black Friday. My eyes flicked down to her purple boots, still bearing faint traces of mud, then veered back to her bright blue eyes.

"I have—just recently, in fact. The bookshelves look great. And the coffee is out of this world. Next time, I hope to visit with the shelter dogs, although I'm not ready to own any animals right now."

Her posture was relaxed, and she didn't seem defensive in the least. I didn't know how to politely ask if she'd dropped in on Black Friday in particular, so I let the matter drop.

"It was nice to see you," I said.

"You too, Macy." I could tell from the way her eyes met mine—wistful and friendly—that she was wondering how I'd report on our interaction to Bo. I'd seen that look on many women's faces over the years, full of hope that I'd build a bridge between them and my brother.

Unfortunately, I'd never had a good grip on what Bo was looking for. He used to be attracted to really independent, driven women like his ex-fiancée, Tara. Once she dumped him because she chose to believe a lying coworker over my infinitely honest brother, I wasn't sure how much of his heart was left for another woman. Tara's "scorched-earth campaign," as I liked to call it, had left precious little in its wake.

However, I still held out hopes that Summer—gentle Summer, our ex-Mennonite shelter director—could make some inroads with Bo. Therefore, I couldn't really offer Sheldia any encouragement in that regard.

I waved her off and headed back inside with Bo, who was walking my way. He looked tired as he asked, "Where'd you disappear to? I was about to shoot you a text."

"Just outside, talking with Sheldia," I said. "Did you have a good chat with Chevy?"

"I did. He's a really down-home guy, but he's more talented than any of the California builders I've worked with."

I waited for him to settle into the driver's seat of his truck before asking, "Sheldia went to school with you, didn't she?"

He nodded. "Sheldia's home life wasn't good. Her dad drank heavily, and when our eighth grade year started, her mom took off and left her kids behind. I think Sheldia's grandparents took them in for a while, then maybe they eventually got shuttled into the foster system."

Now I could see why Sheldia was working hard to become a foster parent and trying to get the Bookmobile back in operation for kids who couldn't make it to the library.

"She got bullied." Bo spoke into the darkened truck interior, which felt pleasantly safe and warm. He gave the truck more gas as we climbed the same hill where the armored truck had skidded over the side. "It was for being dirty, although anyone with a brain knew she couldn't do a blessed thing about it. Every time I caught someone mocking her, I shut them down fast."

No *wonder* Sheldia was nursing a decades-old crush on Bo. He had been her knight in shining armor, time and time again.

"Hey, Bo," I said, hesitant to try out my new theory. "You know how Sheldia said some benefactor donated all that money for the new bus and the foster backpacks?"

"Mm-hm." He kept his eyes on the road, staying quiet until I spoke again.

"Sheldia has purple suede boots, just like the ones I saw on that woman who showed up at the cafe after the wreck," I explained. "Remember how Joe Watkins seemed interested when I mentioned the woman with the muddy boots? What if Sheldia *was* that woman and she was the first to come across the crash scene? She could've checked on the men and realized she couldn't help them, picked up the money, then come back into town to use the pay phone to call for help before anyone saw a thing."

"It wouldn't be a speedy process," Bo said thoughtfully. "Stopping the car, then picking your way down that hill in the ice and snow...you'd have to be pretty sure-footed. Plus, that day the roads were busier, so chances are someone would've noticed a stopped car and offered help."

"Especially an eyesore like her old minivan," I murmured. "Yeah, I guess you're right. I just had the fleeting idea that maybe Sheldia stole the money and donated it to the library."

Bo pulled in front of my house and parked. He gave a short

laugh. "I can't see Sheldia Powers doing anything so personally incriminating. She prefers to fly under the radar."

I pushed back. "Not tonight, she didn't. She was up there giving her spiel about the state of the Bookmobile, and I have to say, she struck me as really impassioned. Maybe she's changed over the years, Bo. Goodness knows I have."

He walked around and opened my door. In the streetlight, I caught a glimpse of sadness in his eyes. "I hate that Jake disillusioned you so much, sis. He was a scoundrel, and I should've realized it a lot sooner."

"None of us did." I followed Bo up the garden path to my back door. When he took out the key, Coal's deep barks reverberated in the living room. Bo opened the door and Coal careened past him, sliding into a stop at my legs as if sensing where I stood.

"Take a walk, you cute punk," I said, pushing him toward the porch stairs so he could go out and relieve himself. I bumped into Bo's arm. "At least cats use the litter box."

"Ah, but then you get to scoop litter all the time," he said.

"Good point."

Coal didn't take long to come rushing back, this time prodding Bo's hand so he'd be inclined to scratch his long nose. "You've got a good dog. I'm always relieved to know he's here for you when I can't be."

I stepped into my living room and gave a short whistle. Coal ambled inside with me. "You coming in for a while, bro?"

Bo shook his head. "I need to talk to some coffee bean suppliers in Guatemala—they're a couple hours behind us and I promised to call before it got too late."

"Okay. Thanks for taking me along to the town council meeting. I found it...interesting."

He chuckled. "You're not too convincing, but hopefully at the very least you got some ideas for Girl's Day Out."

"I did," I assured him.

He said goodnight and jumped off the back steps, exactly the same way he used to do as a teen. For a forty-one-year old man, he seemed to have endless supplies of energy. Meanwhile, at thirty-seven, I'd experienced the kinds of subtle shifts that let me know time was marching forward, and it wasn't going to cut me any breaks.

After closing and locking the door, I kicked off my boots, pulled off my socks, and slid into my worn frog slippers. I brewed hot water and poured a cup of instant hot cocoa. Grabbing a peanut butter cookie I'd brought home from the cafe, I settled into my couch and flipped on the TV. I mindlessly scrolled through several Alaskan wilderness shows —one of my major weaknesses—until my phone buzzed. It was Bristol.

"What's up?" I asked, hoping it was nothing serious.

"I think I'll need to stick around here tomorrow, so I'll need someone to fill in for me," she said. "Ethan's dialysis has gone a little sideways, because he got too dehydrated. They're saying he really needs that kidney transplant, sooner rather than later, but I'm not a match because Ethan and I have different blood and tissue types. Mom can't donate since her kidneys are older. It can take years for a kidney transplant, so we're stuck dealing with what we have right now."

Bristol sounded utterly defeated.

"Have you eaten yet?" I asked. An empty stomach made everything worse.

"Uh, no. I grabbed a couple bites of Ethan's uneaten mashed potatoes, but I haven't been able to get home. It's okay—"

"Listen. I'm going to bring you some food. Is your mom still at work?"

"Yes. She doesn't get home until late."

"Well, I'll bring food and she can grab hers whenever. I'm happy to swing by. What room are you in?"

I hung up and immediately placed an order for take-out, since most restaurants would soon be closing for the night. Coal nuzzled into my hand, probably sensing I was going to have to head out again.

"Sorry, boy. I was hoping to hang out with you, too." I knew I shouldn't be taking on so much responsibility for Bristol and her family, but they'd been hit hard lately. Maybe I needed to talk to the ladies at church about setting up a meal schedule to cover the next couple of weeks for the Goddards. Those ladies truly had the gift of serving others. They were always happy to help the needy in the community.

Summer called when I was heading out to pick up the food. "Are we still on for tomorrow?" she asked.

It had totally slipped my mind that I'd promised Summer we could go to the Greenbrier Resort tomorrow. We were planning to have lunch and chat about plans for Girl's Day Out. It was something I needed to keep on my agenda.

"Of course. I was going to cover for Bristol, but I'll see if someone else can do it."

I hung up and called Jimmy, who was only too happy to fill in for me with the dogs. As I pulled into the hospital, I allowed myself a moment of excitement that I'd get to visit the Greenbrier with Summer. I'd worked in one of their art colony shops for a couple of summers, and I always loved walking around the beautiful grounds, even when there were no flowers out.

Grabbing the pizza boxes—I'd figured pizza would easily feed people for a couple of days and it was easy to transport—I opened my car door and hesitated. Scanning the parking lot, I didn't spot any dark cars with someone lurking inside. Relieved that the blond man must've given up his stalking for now, I headed into the hospital and found Ethan's room, which was on a different floor from his uncle.

Bristol looked weary in her post next to her brother's bed, and Ethan seemed to be resting. I leaned in and pointed to the pizza. Bristol nodded, stepping out into the hall.

"Let's head into the snack room where we can talk," she said. Once inside, she grabbed a paper towel and took a couple pieces of pizza. "This looks so great," she said. "Please have one."

"No, I'm good—I already ate," I said.

She took a bite and munched thoughtfully. "I'm sure this is getting annoying—having to bring me food all the time. You really don't have to."

"No way. Listen, you guys are in a difficult place right now. You can't control your uncle's coma or your brother's health, and your mom has to keep working. You're doing the right thing, being here for Ethan."

She sank into a chair. "I know, but I'm eternally grateful to you. I know my mom and brother are, too."

"How's your uncle?" I asked.

"To be honest, I haven't had time to check on him today," she said, wiping her mouth. "Mom texted earlier and said nothing had changed, though."

"How about I go up and check on him?" I figured it might put Bristol's mind at ease...but I also wanted to scan the halls for the blond Germanic man.

Bristol's eyes brightened. "Sure, that would be great. The nurses are supposed to call Mom if he wakes up, but this way, I could tell her you were able to see him."

I hopped up. "I'll do that now," I said.

I took the elevator to Clark's floor and strode toward his room, giving a nod to the nurse on duty who had seen me before.

I peered in the door, which was slightly ajar, and stopped in my tracks.

Inside the room, a short man was adjusting a balloon bouquet on Clark's bedside table. I realized at once that it was Les Stevens, owner of Stevens Security. What was he doing here this time of night?

9

LES THREW furtive glances around the room, so I drew back in the doorway, hoping he couldn't see me. When I peeked back in, he had pulled out his phone and was staring at the screen. I couldn't see what he was looking at, but next thing I knew, he was carefully rearranging the balloon bouquet.

This time, he turned so his phone screen was facing me. I sucked in my breath when I saw what he was looking at.

His screen showed Clark, lying on his bed. There had to be a hidden camera in that bouquet. From the angle of the feed, I was betting the camera was in the bottom of the vase.

He gave a satisfied nod and headed toward the door, so I skedaddled down the hall, glancing around frantically for a place to hide. A small bathroom door stood open, so I darted into it and locked the door behind me. After five minutes had passed, I cracked the door and looked out, but Les Stevens wasn't around.

Fighting the urge to march straight into Clark's room, grab the vase, and throw it into a dumpster, I gave Detective Hatcher a call instead. I knew enough to know that Les' fingerprints would be all over the vase—and quite possibly the camera, which had to be illegal. The detective and I agreed that Les must be watching for any signs of movement from Clark, so he'd be the first to know if he woke from his coma.

The question was *why*? Was Les so convinced that Clark was involved in stealing 500 grand? How did he figure Clark managed to do that before slipping into a coma? Things just didn't add up, but one thing that seemed abundantly clear was that Les was willing to work the wrong side of the law to get what he wanted.

Detective Hatcher said someone was on the way to pick up the camera, and he asked if I could stick around and watch the room until then. I agreed, but I didn't want Les to see I came in right after him, so I stood outside the room, hopefully outside the camera's line of sight.

Sure enough, an officer dropped by to bag up the vase and balloons. Throughout the unusual hubbub in his room, Clark didn't move one iota. He certainly wasn't faking a coma. Could that be what Les was afraid of—that Clark might be scamming his company somehow?

Bristol texted me to see if everything was okay. I didn't want to worry her with news of Les' thwarted spying attempt, so I said I'd been in the bathroom, but that Clark hadn't moved or changed. I told her I was heading home and asked if I should stop downstairs to see her first, but she said she was fine. She was going to stay in the chair next to Ethan until her mom arrived later in the night.

I was glad to hear that Della was going to be around, although I figured things were safe enough, because Les Stevens probably wouldn't show up twice in the same night. Detective Hatcher said he'd have the night staff watch for Les and ban him from visiting Clark's room again. I knew the detective would let Della know the moment he picked Les up for questioning about the secret video camera.

Once I got home and parked the car, I took a deep, bracing breath as I pushed open the gate to my back garden. The brisk air smelled of woodsmoke, and it carried a sharp tinge that whispered snow was coming tonight. It was a rough time of year for Della and Bristol to be making trips to the hospital, and I hoped against hope Clark would wake from his coma...maybe in time for Christmas. Or that Ethan would get a kidney donor before then.

Coal shoved his warm, happy face against me as I opened the door. I wondered how I'd gotten through those eight years in South Carolina without a dog. I supposed I'd repressed a lot of my disappointments during that time...or maybe I hadn't truly allowed myself to feel them as long as I told myself Jake loved me.

I rubbed Coal's head. "Thanks for waiting up, boy. I'm done for the day. Let me get my PJs on, then we're going to relax."

I never failed to give a happy sigh as I walked past the white pillars into the front door of the Greenbrier Resort. From the green carpet to the ivory metal chandelier to the paintings on the walls, everything felt high-class. Summer waited just inside the door, and I noted that both she and I had dressed up for the occasion. She'd pulled her hair up and wore a long velvet skirt, a velvet choker, and a flowing white blouse. With her boots and maroon lipstick, she looked like she'd stepped out of the nineties, but I didn't tell her that.

Meanwhile, I probably looked a little too springy in my poppy print blouse, tailored pants, and bright red headband. I was able to pull off colors like hot pink and some shades of red, even with my strawberry blonde hair, because my eyes were somewhere between blue and gray and my skin was quite fair. Auntie A had steadfastly maintained that redheads should stick to deep blue and green shades—and Bo had certainly taken that advice—but darker colors always seemed to overpower me.

Summer gave me a ridiculous air kiss, and I grinned, returning it.

"So we're feeling posh today, are we, *dahling*?" I asked.

She linked her arm in mine and steered me toward Draper's, a restaurant decorated largely in pink and green florals as an homage to Dorothy Draper, the woman who'd concocted the resort's bright and eclectic interior design scheme.

"I don't know about you, but I'm having the fried green tomato sandwich," Summer said, sliding into a booth.

"I'm a sucker for their Reuben," I said, pulling a small notebook from my clutch. "Okay, let's order and get down to planning."

The server came over and took our order, then returned quickly with our sweet teas.

I took a sip. "Did you have any ideas for Girl's Day Out?"

Summer fiddled with the pendant on her choker, which I realized was a tiny silver cat. "Yes, I do. You know how I told you we were trying to recruit more pet foster families, so we could have more animals in homes while they wait for adoption? I was thinking that maybe you all could offer a twenty percent cafe discount to anyone who would sign up to foster pets that day."

I liked her idea. Part of the mission of Barks & Beans had always been to get shelter dogs placed in the right homes, and supporting the shelter's growing foster program could only help.

The server returned, placing our salads in front of us. I

grabbed my fork and loaded up a large bite. "Sure, that would work well. But I feel like we need to offer something else, something not contingent on fostering."

"Of course. How about a gift basket? Lots of stores are doing raffle giveaways. Barks & Beans could have a really eclectic basket—fill it with coffees, teas, and dog-themed items, you know?"

"I love it. If we included a small bag of our house blend, people might want to return for more."

Summer nodded. "Bo's coffee is the best." Her cheeks colored a little, but I pretended not to notice.

WE DECIDED to walk off our meal by checking out the indoor shops. As we passed the Ralph Lauren store, I stepped in the door to gape at the artfully arranged tie display.

"Look at those gorgeous colors. I wonder if I could afford one of those for Bo?" I asked.

Summer shook her head. "I didn't think he liked ties much. Does he even wear them to church?"

"He does occasionally, but you're right. That's an expensive gift he might not even like." Come to think of it, they looked more like something Jake would wear.

Toward the back of the store, something caught my eye. Or rather, some*one*.

The blond Germanic man was holding up polo shirts, talking to someone. I took a step to the left to see who it was.

Joe Watkins, the con man questioner.

This was proof positive those two were in on something together, but what? I turned to Summer. "I need to get closer to those guys," I said. "They're the ones I was telling you about who were asking questions about Bristol and the wreck."

Summer's brown eyes widened and she vehemently shook her head. Grabbing my elbow, she moved us toward the door. "No. We have to get out of here. You told me yourself that the tall guy carries a gun, right? And he's huge. What if he follows us out?"

She did have a point. Maybe this wasn't the time and place to try to get close—the store didn't provide a lot of covert hiding places, especially since we were two females dawdling in the men's section.

"Alright, alright," I whispered, following her out the door. She started speed-walking down the sloped hallway and I caught up with her. "I'd better let Detective Hatcher know they're obviously together and probably up to no good."

She agreed, so we hurried out the side door onto a stone patio, where I stopped and placed my call to the detective. He said he'd have someone confirm that the men were registered at the Greenbrier and find out their names. I asked about Les Stevens, and he said that although they'd gone to his home, he wasn't in, so they hadn't been able to question him about the hidden video camera. Oddly, he hadn't shown up for work today, either.

Something was definitely off about Les Stevens. As Summer and I walked along the grounds to where we'd parked, I told her about Les and the hidden camera.

"Was I wrong to keep that from Della?" I asked. "It's just that they have so much going on with Della's brother in a coma and her son's kidney disease."

"No, you weren't," Summer said firmly. "The cops are going to find Les and question him about it. Maybe he got the wind up when his video feed got interrupted—presumably by a cop, right? And maybe he didn't want to get hauled in and asked about it, so he ran."

"Which would seem to indicate he's involved in something underhanded," I said.

Summer looked thoughtful. "Do you think he was somehow involved in the heist?"

"Robbing one of his own trucks?" I asked. "That doesn't make sense. Like Bo told me, Les has every reason to want that $500,000 to be recovered. Otherwise, his entire security company looks bad."

"True. And why would he spy on Clark if he already had the money?"

"Good point. I just have this feeling I'm missing something, maybe something the cops overlooked." Heavy snowflakes started falling, coating my hair and tickling my nose. "We'd better book it back before the roads get bad," I said. "I'm going to keep thinking on things."

Summer laughed. "You do that, Scooby-Doo. Unravel the mystery."

I grinned. "Somebody has to."

10

By the time I got home, the snow was tapering off, leaving the ground wet but not coated. After changing into my beat-up jeans and a flannel shirt, I donned my coat and gloves and headed into the back yard with Coal. I wanted to check in my gardening shed and bag up the irises I'd lifted for Summer and Jimmy.

As I dropped the cold bulbs into paper bags, my thoughts returned to the two men at the Greenbrier. Those men had to be looking for the money that had gone missing from the truck, given the questions they'd been asking.

But what role did Les play? Why did he seem to be in the middle of things?

Coal was lying with his body stretched along the length of the shed door, but he refused to take one step inside. I figured his shed phobia stemmed from the small building he'd been hidden in last month when he'd been dognapped.

It was not a pleasant memory for either of us.

I grabbed the stuffed bags, then reached down and patted

Coal's head. "Let's go, big boy. I won't stay in here any longer than I have to."

As he launched to his feet and pressed against my side, I pulled off my gloves and gave Jimmy a call.

"The dogs are doing great today, Miss Hatfield," he assured me. "How's Bristol?"

I realized I hadn't checked in with her yet, so after telling Jimmy I'd drop the bulbs by the cafe in a bit, I hung up and called Bristol.

"Things are looking up," she said. "Ethan's getting much stronger and he's ready to go home, but they have to keep him overnight until his levels are where they need to be. I've been hanging out with him, but he's insisting I go home and go to bed early, so I probably will. And don't even ask if I need food—we still have leftover pizza in the fridge, thanks to you."

"Good, and I agree about going to bed early. You need to get rest as much as anyone. Is your mom working today?"

"She's actually sitting with someone later tonight, but she's going to pick me up first."

I knew Bristol wasn't a child, but I felt a little worried for her, being home alone. "Call me if you need anything, okay? I'm happy to come right over."

"Thank you, Miss Hatfield. I'm sure I'll be fine, but I'll keep that in mind."

Coal's barks roused me from a deep sleep around one thirty in the morning. I rolled over, feeling for the lamp switch, only to see my phone had lit up with a call. I'd forgotten to turn the ringer on, so it must've been vibrating, which was probably why Coal was trying to alert me.

I saw it was Bristol, so I picked up quickly. "What's—"

"Miss Hatfield," she said, her voice raspy. "Someone broke in."

I sat straight up. *"What?"*

She seemed to catch her breath, like she'd been running. Had she left her house?

"I...called the police. But could you come to my house until they get here?"

I didn't ask questions. "I'll be there in five."

As soon as I hung up, I called Bo, who said he'd be over in a minute to pick me up.

I'd only had time to pull on a pair of jeans and throw a coat over my pajama top when I saw his truck lights on the street. I gave Coal a pat and rushed out to meet my brother.

We said next to nothing on the way over, but we were both more alert than anyone should have been at that time of night.

"Did you get your gun?" I asked.

"You know it," he said.

I didn't even ask which gun—knowing Bo, he could be toting an entire arsenal under that bulky barn coat. Bo was like a one-man army as far as backup went.

The Goddards' house was mostly dark, so I wondered again if Bristol had stayed inside or made a run for it. I assumed she'd be watching for us.

When I gave a light knock on the door, a curtain shifted a little, then we heard the locks turn. Bristol opened the door and leaned against the doorframe. She wore rumpled sweats and a tank top, and her hair was disheveled. She was still a little breathy as she asked us to come in, and I noticed her face was flushed.

She eased onto the couch as if movement was taxing for her. She motioned to a cup of water that sat on the side table, and I handed it to her.

"Do you mind if I check over the house?" Bo asked.

She motioned him on, then took a drink of water and pointed to her neck. "Someone choked me, then they ran," she explained.

"They choked you?" I repeated. "Why? What were they doing in your house?"

"I don't know. I woke up because I heard a noise in the living room, like a drawer closing. I figured I'd just imagined it, because I'd locked both doors and checked them twice. I got up to check things out, and I saw this guy with a flashlight in the kitchen. I was about to run to my room and grab my phone, but someone snuck up on me. He wrapped an arm around my neck and got me in a rear choke hold. I was out like a light. But thank goodness he didn't strangle me or something."

"Did you see either of them?" I asked.

She nodded, taking another sip of water. "The guy in the kitchen was about my height and had dark hair, from what I could tell. I have no idea what the man behind me looked like, but he must've been tall because I think he was reaching down to choke me."

"Were you out for long?" I asked, concerned.

"I don't know, but when I got up, they were both gone. I figured they must've come in through the kitchen window. It doesn't really lock properly—Mom's been meaning to get it fixed for a while."

I was betting that window lock repair would jump to the top of Della's To-Do list in a hurry. "Have you called your mom?" I asked.

"No. I knew you were coming, and the police are, too. I don't want her stressing at work."

I disagreed, knowing if I were Bristol's mom, I'd want to know immediately what had happened. If Bristol wouldn't let her know about the break-in and attack, then I would.

Bo returned to the living room after doing a quick, but

thorough once-over of the small house. "No one's here now," he said. "I caught the tail end of what you were saying—so someone choked you?"

The doorbell rang before Bristol could answer, startling all of us. Bo strode over and shoved the curtain aside. "It's the police," he said, opening the door.

Detective Hatcher walked in, his look serious. He nodded at Bo and me, then his gaze fixed on Bristol. "Are you okay, miss?"

Bristol gave a slight nod before slumping back against the couch. "I'm just kind of tired, that's all."

Knowing the girl didn't feel like talking, I jumped in and shared Bristol's account with the detective. One of the police officers checked her pulse and breathing before announcing that she was okay, but needed to lie down and rest.

"You can't stay here alone." My voice was firm. "And the police will be dusting for prints for a while. How about if you come back to my place—I have a spare room—and I'll let your mom know what's going on. You know there's no way she'd want you here by yourself, either."

Bristol gave a weak nod, so Bo helped her to her feet. As she was pulling on her coat and shoes, I walked over to Detective Hatcher.

"A regular height dark-haired man and a taller man...they fit the description of the two at the Greenbrier today," I said.

"Yes. But we found out they're no longer registered there. They *had* been, but they checked out this morning. The good news is that now we know their names. However, the bad news is that one of them is from overseas, so things might be delayed as we check with his government."

Had the international man traveled all the way to the US just to knock off an armored truck in rural West Virginia? That didn't make sense, although $500,000 was a substantial amount of money.

"Do you think they were in cahoots with someone?" I asked. "Like Clark or Christian?"

The detective's face was grim. "It seems like a long shot, but stranger things have happened."

I mused aloud. "Maybe the international guy and his friend planned to stop and 'rob' the truck, but then it hit black ice and their cohorts were out of commission. By the time they crawled down the hill, Clark could've hidden the money from them...somehow?"

I hated to think of Clark being involved, but it was possible, given his sister's financial needs. Then there was Les and his mysterious behavior...

Bo stepped back into the house. "Bristol's in the truck," he said. "We'd better get her back so she can rest."

The detective took a deep breath and slowly released it. "Alrighty. I'll let you know if we find any definite prints, but I have a feeling those two will be getting out of Dodge, money or no money. They aren't going to be able to stick around town—we'll be pressing charges as soon as we clear it internationally, and I'm probably going to put out a warrant on Les Stevens, too. He's simply not responding to any of our efforts to contact him. We'll be working here to wrap things up tonight, and there'll be at least one unit outside until tomorrow morning. Try not to worry."

I followed Bo onto the darkened street, considering what the detective had said. It was hard not to worry. Greed was a powerful motivator, and I was betting the two burglars wouldn't actually leave until they found the stash—especially if one of them had flown to the U.S. just to steal the money.

Someone had taken that cash, and these men were hunting for it.

The question was, who *was* that someone? Clark seemed an impossible suspect because he was in a coma. Christian was dead. And although Les seemed suspicious, it hardly seemed likely he'd torpedo his own security business by risking a truck heist.

I thought back to Black Friday. Sheldia was the only suspicious person in the cafe that day, and she certainly didn't seem like someone who would've done a snatch-and-grab at the scene of the crash.

Or was she?

Della was upset to hear that the men had broken into her house, then completely horrified to learn one of them had choked her daughter. I assured her that Bristol had been checked out and just needed to rest, so I was taking her to my place.

Della waffled around, torn between her commitment to her employer and her desire to rush home to be with her oldest. I managed to put her mind at ease by reminding her that Coal was a good guard dog and that no one would suspect Bristol was staying with me. Plus, what if Ethan crashed or Clark woke up and she had to rush over to the hospital?

After having a brief conversation with Bristol, who was snuggled into my guest room bed, Della finally gave the go-ahead for her to stay. I couldn't imagine what a trying time this was for the hard-working single mom.

I brought Bristol a cup of homemade cocoa with spray whip and cinnamon sprinkles on top, my comfort drink of choice. Her eyelids were heavy and she was practically dozing off. I glanced at my phone and realized it was past three in the morning. After pulling Bristol's door shut, I headed into the hallway, where Coal was lying on the floor as if too exhausted to follow me around.

I walked around him and gave a light whistle. "Sorry, boy. It's time for bed again."

Coal yawned and plodded into the room behind me. He completely ditched his pillow-kneading routine, instead dropping onto it like a sack of potatoes.

"Long day," I breathed, trying to plump my own pillow into a comfortable position. But sleep was elusive, and some part of my body seemed to be stuck in fight-or-flight mode. Usually, when I was all wound up like this, I'd walk on the treadmill or in town to burn off my restless energy. But those options were impossible this time of night, especially with Bristol asleep in the next room.

Instead, I grabbed my phone and turned on an audiobook. For some reason, listening to someone reading always calmed my worries. As the male narrator with a liquid voice talked about car chases and spy adventures, I finally drifted off to sleep.

11

I woke to the tantalizing smells of eggs, bacon, and fresh-brewed coffee. I stepped into my green slippers and headed downstairs, with Coal close on my heels.

He bypassed me and headed straight toward Bristol, who was standing next to the stove. She flipped a couple of pieces of bacon, then turned toward me. "I slept so well," she said, politely nudging Coal aside when he edged too close to the pan on the stovetop. "And today my neck feels a lot better. I made breakfast for you, since you're always making me food. Now, where do you keep your dishes?"

I opened the cabinet and pulled out a couple plates. Glancing at the microwave clock, I felt a little jolt. It was already seven.

"I'd better eat fast and let Bo know I'm coming in," I said.

Bristol shook her head. "I've already called and worked everything out—I'm on Barks duty at the cafe today." She held a hand up, anticipating my protest. "I know you're going to tell me not to, but I need to feel like I'm accomplishing something other than sitting around in hospitals. I'll be safe at the cafe; no one's going to sneak up on me there. I've already talked to Kylie, and she's filling in for me until I can run home to get my clothes changed."

"But you're still recuperating from the trauma of last night," I said.

She set her jaw. "Hanging out with the shelter dogs will be just the therapy I need. I know you understand."

Her brown eyes were winsome, and I had to admit that I did completely understand. Dogs were a good cure for many things. "Have you talked to your mom about this plan?" I asked.

"Yes, she texted me around six, so I asked her then. She's okay with it. Thankfully, Ethan's doing better, and he's going to be released today. Mom's going to pick him up around ten."

"Okay. Let me finish this last bite of egg, then I'll run you to your house for clothes," I said. "Thank you for the excellent breakfast." I swirled a laden forkful in the air before plunging it into my mouth.

Bristol held my gaze. "It's the very least I can do, believe me. You've been a lifesaver for my family this entire week. I'll never forget how you stepped in to help."

It was a kind sentiment, but I was still convinced I could do more. I just wasn't sure *what*.

AFTER DROPPING by Bristol's house so she could get dressed and touch base with Della, I drove her to Barks & Beans and waited until she got in the door. As I pulled out, I smiled as I always did at the sight of the cheery red-and-white awnings over the front windows. I made a mental note that it was time to pick up new wreaths, lights, and other decorations to add some seasonal flair. Part of Lewisburg's charm was the way the shops got all "gussied up" for Christmas.

I drove around the cafe and pulled into a parking space along the sidewalk. Anxious to act on an idea I'd had on the way home, I jogged up to my door. Once inside, I grabbed gloves and a hat before hitching Coal to his leash and walking him into the back garden. After he'd done his business in the yard, I thrilled him by opening the gate and walking him onto the sidewalk. I led him to my car and opened the passenger door, where I cranked the passenger seat back as far as possible. When I motioned him to get inside, he gave an anxious yawn, but I repeated my command.

Taking car rides with Coal was always an interesting proposition. It was much easier to load my one hundred and sixty-five pound dog into Bo's truck, but this time I'd decided Bo didn't need to know what I was up to.

Coal tentatively placed first one front paw, then the other on the passenger floorboard. Once he managed to get his back paws to follow suit, he attempted to circle his new domain. When that proved impossible, he determined his best option was to place his rump squarely on the floorboard, so he was facing me. He draped his front paws and torso across the passenger seat, shooting me a resigned look that said although my human foibles were infinitely tiring, he was willing to endure them this *one* time.

After making sure Coal's tail wasn't hanging out, I closed the door and headed around to the driver's seat. Thankful it wasn't a long drive to my destination, I started the engine and pulled out, accidentally bopping Coal's head a couple of times. He sighed and lowered his head to the center console.

The one stone I'd left unturned was to travel to the actual location where the armored truck had wrecked. While I knew the police must have scoured the area, I was convinced there was something they were missing at the crash site. Like Bo had said, Clark was local, and Christian was from Summers

County. They were familiar with the roads around here, so they *knew* to watch for black ice on top of that particular hill.

"I'm not stupid enough to think I'm going to find the hidden bank stash," I said aloud to Coal, whose ears were turned my way. "But let's see if we can retrace their steps, shall we?"

As I slowly topped the dangerous hill, I noted tire skid marks that angled directly toward a smashed-down section of guardrail. A fluttering remnant of police tape left no doubt as to where the heavy truck had skidded off the road.

I pulled off at the first graveled turnabout I saw, which was likely the exact place the female good Samaritan had stopped on Black Friday. The road was relatively quiet, so I leashed Coal and hauled him out with me. He trotted close to my side as we crossed the road, then we hiked the short distance to the battered guardrail.

I braced myself before taking a look over the side of the hill. I had known the incline was steep, but it was shocking to see what a precipitous drop it was to the forest floor below. It was clear where the vehicle had come to rest, because a couple of trees had been snapped over, and metal pieces lay strewn on the ground nearby.

How had someone clambered down a straight drop like that, especially with ice and snow on the ground? I glanced over the side again and shuddered. There was just no way. The mystery woman would've needed a climbing rope and spikes for her boots.

I led Coal down to a curve in the road, where the road widened. It was almost directly across from the roundabout where I'd parked. This was clearly the best entry point to climb to the forest floor below. There were plenty of smaller trees to hold onto, and there weren't as many rocks as there were higher up.

Reluctantly, I walked Coal back to the car and positioned

him in the passenger seat again. "Sorry, boy, but you can't make it down there with me, and if I leash you to a tree, someone could easily grab you. I promise I'll be as fast as I can."

I went back to my car seat and cracked all the windows, although in the chilly weather, Coal didn't run any risk of suffocation. I got out and hit the lock button, then checked to make sure it had worked. A vehicle slowly passed by—probably wondering if I was in trouble—and I gave a brief and hopefully carefree wave. Once it had rounded the next curve, I dashed across the road and started my descent to the forest floor.

Luckily, I'd spent a lot of time in the woods, so finding my footing wasn't too hard. The ground was still a little wet from the recent snow, and I tried to imagine how messy it would've been on Black Friday.

I reminded myself that it wasn't a foregone conclusion that the woman who'd called emergency services had been the one to steal the $500,000. Maybe she'd just noticed the crash as she drove down the hill—for instance, maybe the damaged truck was smoking. She could've pulled over, turned around, then headed back into town to place her call.

In the meantime, someone else could've come along and robbed the truck's exposed cache. It would've taken time and some persistence, but if they recognized it as an armored security truck, it might've been tempting.

My worn boot soles slipped when I stepped on a thick pile of leaves the truck must've churned up on its way down. I managed not to fall—for some reason, I'd been blessed with a very solid sense of balance. Sadly, I'd never been able to use it to become a dazzling cheerleader, gymnast, or ballerina, since my overall coordination left much to be desired. Maybe I was a little like Coal in that way.

As if we were connected on some mental plane, Coal gave a pitiful yowl from the car. I focused on the task at hand, setting to work searching the area the truck had flattened. Aside from the pieces of twisted metal lying around, I found nothing. I made a brief search for any hollowed tree trunks or logs where the money could've been hidden, but my gut told me there'd be nothing left since the police combed over everything. I did discover a fallen log toward the perimeter of the crash site, but it was still mostly solid inside. There was no way anyone could've stuffed twenty pounds' worth of bills in it.

Coal started barking as I picked my way back up the tree-lined incline. Whoever took the money must have had a bag to carry it in, otherwise they would've spent most of their time retrieving flyaway bills as they attempted scaling the snowy steep bank.

When I reached the car, Coal whined and scratched at the door. I was fairly certain he needed a bathroom break before we headed home, so I clicked his leash in place and led him toward the sandstone face of the mountain. Once he was finished, he eagerly began sniffing along some invisible trail that wound between pieces of litter. I pulled his leash tighter, and he responded by slowing down and heeling. He was such a large dog, he could've easily taken off and dragged me, but thankfully he had been trained to be considerate of his owner.

He suddenly came to an abrupt stop and shoved his nose into a yellowed patch of weeds. Before I could pull him back, he'd retrieved something and was holding it delicately between his huge teeth. It looked like some kind of insulated thermos.

"Drop it." I pointed to the ground.

His teeth still held his treasure as he gave me a forlorn stare, as if I'd taken away his only reason for living.

I took a step closer. "Coal, you know exactly what I said. Drop it *now*."

This time, he obeyed and dropped it like a hot potato. It

rolled until it came to a stop by my tire, exposing a pink monogram on the green plaid insulated cup portion.

Hoping to examine it more closely, I loaded Coal into his seat. A red truck slowed as it approached the turnaround, and I knew I needed to be on my way soon. Leaning down toward the thermos, I was taken by surprise when the truck pulled in directly behind my car.

A younger man with a brown beard, cap, and kind blue eyes rolled down his window. "Ma'am, do you need help? I saw you on my way down a while ago."

I could tell he was a local, someone who didn't mean me any harm. "Thank you, but I'm fine. I'm just looking for something."

He nodded and tipped his head. "Okay, then." As his truck pulled onto the road, I realized why he looked familiar—he was little Billy Keaton, all grown up. I babysat him a few times when his family lived down the road from us. They had later moved to another part of town, but I'd never forget Billy's high-wire antics.

One night after I'd put him to bed, I'd heard some thudding upstairs. When I went up to check, I heard Billy humming to himself...sitting on the low roof outside his second-story window. He had a flashlight and Matchbox cars and was playing out there like it was his nightly bedtime routine. His mom later reassured me that this wasn't his first venture onto that roof.

It was certainly comforting to know that little Billy had survived to adulthood, and that he'd turned into a gentleman, to boot. Come to think of it, he *had* given me a long second glance, so he'd probably recognized me, too. I hadn't changed all that much. Maybe he'd felt a pang of embarrassment over his roof expedition, but I hoped not.

Brushing those amusing memories aside, I grabbed a stick

and rolled the thermos so I could make out the curling monogram. It was clearly of high quality, and since it was monogrammed, it didn't seem like something anyone would've wanted to throw out.

The initials said "DGB." My stomach clenched.

Surely the one person I knew with those initials wouldn't have been hanging out in the parking space across from where the armored truck crashed...and surely she wouldn't have had anything to do with the $500,000 that went missing.

Della Beth Goddard.

12

I USED a tissue to carefully pick up the thermos and place it in my back seat. Although I knew I needed to give it to the police, I wasn't in any rush to do so. There were any number of perfectly reasonable explanations as to why Della's thermos could've been tossed along the road in this particular spot...weren't there? And maybe I was wrong about the pink initials—surely there could be other women in town with the same ones?

Once I pulled up at home and opened Coal's car door, he came tumbling out, anxious to burn off his pent-up energy. I unleashed him in the back garden and let him run while I sat down on one of the rickety lawn chairs on my back porch and surveyed the slumbering flowerbeds.

It'd be great if Bo and I could expand my porch and fix it up sometime. Maybe I could even hire Chevy for the job, once I saved up the money. It shouldn't take long, because I was basically living rent-free. Bo owned Auntie A's house, and he wouldn't think of charging me a cent to live in it.

I also needed outdoor furniture where I could relax and

watch Coal play around the garden in summer. I leaned back, dreaming about my magazine-worthy new porch, but my chair creaked and nearly toppled backward. I slammed my feet to the ground and caught my breath.

The hard smack of reality forced my thoughts right back to Della. I didn't want to hand the thermos over to Detective Hatcher because I didn't want to take Della seriously as a suspect in this heist.

Yet as I considered people with a good motive for stealing a large sum of money, Della would have to top the list. She was a single mom working long hours to make ends meet, all the while caring for a chronically ill teen *who needed a kidney transplant*.

That was the sticking point for me. Any mom would be desperate to find a kidney for her child, especially when she wasn't a match herself. And, if most TV shows were to be believed, money had the power to move you up the transplant list faster.

Had Della planned the heist ahead of time? Maybe she'd attempted to stop the truck, not realizing the ice would cause it to swerve right over the bank. However, that seemed far too careless a move for a woman who obviously loved her brother. On top of that, she'd dated Christian. I couldn't see how she'd endanger either of them.

Maybe when the truck had skidded and crashed, Clark had managed to call his sister before he blacked out. If that had been the scenario, I was sure Della would've come running, only to realize there was nothing she could do to revive her brother or Christian. She might've noticed the cash and decided to shove some into her purse before climbing up and heading into town to place an anonymous call for help. In her hurry, she could've knocked the thermos out of her car.

Coal bounded up the steps and contentedly planted his

nose on my lap. I stroked his soft fur, wishing I felt half as carefree.

But I knew what I needed to do.

I picked up my phone and called Della.

SHE ANSWERED RIGHT AWAY, her voice unusually bright. It took me a moment to remember that Ethan was probably home from the hospital now.

"How's Ethan?" I asked.

I could hear her smiling on the other end. "He's doing so much better, thanks. It's nice to see he's hydrated, so he'll be ready for his next dialysis. But what's up? Bristol's doing okay, isn't she? I wasn't sure about letting her go in today—"

"She's fine," I reassured her. "Yes, she was determined to go in and hang out with the dogs. I think you were right to let her do it."

Della sighed. "Oh, good. I can't tell you how many times I miss having their father around to ask for advice."

Sympathy for the widow washed over me. "I'm sure." I steeled myself for what I needed to do. "Listen, Della, I had a strange question for you."

"Oh really? What's that?"

"Are you missing a monogrammed thermos, by any chance?"

"Hang on a sec," she said, her keys clacking together. "I'll check."

I heard doors opening and closing. Finally, Della said, "You know what, I think I *did* lose my thermos. It was a nice one, too."

"What's it look like?" I knew exactly what she was going to say.

"It's green plaid with pink monogramming."

Coal was dozing at my feet, but I leaned over and petted his long back, just to feel more grounded. In response, he gave a grunt and stretched his long limbs, draping his heavy paws over my feet.

To my dismay, my worst suspicions had just been confirmed. Della must've been near the crash site on Black Friday. Now what should I do?

I decided to keep things vague. "I found it along the road today, and I noticed it had your initials, so I thought I'd ask."

She sounded curious. "Really? Where?"

There was no way to play down the significance of the locale unless I lied, and that was always a bad plan of action. Auntie A used to tell me if I "planted the wind, I'd reap the whirlwind" when it came to lying, and after some childhood trial and error, I'd discovered she was right.

I took a deep breath. "Actually, I found it near the cliff where your brother crashed."

She paused. When she spoke again, her voice was flat. "You don't say."

Noting her change of tone, I pressed her. "Della, please tell me you weren't anywhere near the crash site on Black Friday."

Her response was quick. "I was, but I didn't tell the police. Now, please hear me out. It was nothing but a strange coincidence, I swear. I was heading over to sit with one of my patients, and as I came around the curve, my overnight bag shifted and spilled out onto the floor. My contact solution popped open and started pouring out, so I pulled over in one of those wider roundabouts, opened the side door, and stuffed everything back into the bag. I must've bumped my thermos out of the door's cup holder—it's old and the plastic holder is broken, so cups are always tilting around. I didn't miss it until later, and you can understand why I didn't want to go back to hunt for it. It would look suspicious."

"But the whole *thing* looks suspicious, don't you see?" I asked urgently. "Didn't you notice the wreck? Or did you pull off before it happened?"

"I honestly don't know if it was before or after. I'm telling you, I didn't see a thing," she insisted. "That's why I was so messed up when the police called and told me what happened to Christian and Clark. I hadn't been far from them, so why didn't I notice anything?" She sighed. "I've kicked myself a thousand times for being in such a rush on Friday."

I liked Della, but I was finding her story extremely hard to believe. "So you're saying nothing happened while you were pulled over? Did anyone drive by you?" Coal picked up on my irritated tone and raised his head, giving me an inquisitive look. I gave him a couple of back pats, and he dropped his head to his paws.

"I was bent over stuffing things in my bag, so I really didn't notice any cars going by." After a pause, she said, "Wait—come to think of it, there was a car pulling out of the roundabout just as I pulled in. I think it was a navy four-door. Do you think that's important?"

A navy four-door. Could it be the same dark Hyundai I'd seen in the hospital parking lot?

"Yes, it could be. Listen, I'm going to have to tell the police. It's possible that car had something to do with your brother's crash."

She gasped. "You really think so? But if I pulled off just after they wrecked, that means...it means I might've been there just as Clark slipped into a coma, or even worse, when Christian was dying!" She choked back a sob.

I heard the agony in her voice. "You couldn't have known," I said.

She sniffled. "Oh, heavens to Betsy. You don't mind telling the police what happened? I have to go into work soon, and I need to make sure Ethan's all settled first—"

"Don't worry about it. I'll tell them exactly what you told me. They really need to know about that other car."

DETECTIVE HATCHER DIDN'T RESPOND to my text, so I stood, wondering what to do next. My stomach was rumbling, so I opened the screen door and headed inside. Coal followed me, his tail doing a slow wag. I scooped a little dog food into his bowl before heading to the fridge, where I stood and looked at the barren interior as if I could wish a delicious lunch into existence.

Realizing I could head into the cafe and pick up one of Charity's amazing gourmet sandwiches, I gave Coal a brief head pat, pulled on my boots and coat, and headed out the door. As I closed my garden gate and walked around the house, I glanced over at the empty bay window in my side room, realizing Auntie A would've had a Christmas tree up by this time of year.

I had so many great memories of traipsing out to the Christmas tree farm on our annual tree hunt. Bo and I always had the final say on which one was chosen—but we had to agree. I could see now that Auntie A used that time to force us to talk things through so we could come to a decision we both approved. It was a good training exercise, really.

Bo was in charge of loading the tree and setting it up at home. Auntie A made us all hot chocolate before she and I got busy with the decorations. From that day on, Auntie A faithfully kept the lights burning on the tree from the time she rose in the early morning until late at night. I'd stay up staring at their multi-colored glow...probably wishing for my one true love to come galloping onto the scene in his proverbial shining armor.

I'd definitely been a hopeless romantic back in my teen years. Nowadays, I'd become suspicious of *any* romantic overtures, which was unfortunate. Dylan Butler seemed interested in me, but I was sure my reticence to go on dates had indicated that I wasn't ready to pursue a relationship with him. Hopefully, he didn't feel it was personal, because it certainly wasn't. He was a kind, interesting, and handsome guy, and on top of that, my brother liked him. However, with self-defeating certainty, I knew any guys I dated would eventually run into my protective "It's not you, it's me" wall.

Shaking off my bleak thoughts, I pushed open the cafe door. The normal lunch crowd had dwindled, and Charity and Milo were deep in discussion behind the coffee bar. Bo was dumping coffee grounds, but turned as I walked his way.

He gave me a quick smile and a wink. "Let's see...you're not working today, so I'm guessing you're hungry?"

"You know me too well." I considered telling Bo about my conversation with Della, but a customer walked in and distracted him.

Charity broke away from Milo and reached into the mini fridge, retrieving a package wrapped in wax paper. "You *have* to try this. Let me heat one in the microwave for you."

I plunked onto a barstool. "What is it?"

Without waiting for my approval, Charity placed the sandwich on one of the cafe's deep blue Fiestaware plates, then popped it in the small microwave. "It's a Southwestern BLT with chipotle mayo on a ciabatta roll. It's been selling like hotcakes. This is the last one." She pulled it out, added the mayo, and pushed the plate toward me. "I know you're going to love it."

Milo nodded. "I've already eaten two. You want a fresh cup of house blend, Macy? Er—sorry, I mean Miss Hatfield."

I'd insisted that the younger employees call me Miss Hatfield after Milo had once called me by my first name in the kind of chummy manner that indicated he had zero respect for the fact that I was his boss.

"Sure, I'd love one, thanks." It was encouraging to see Milo, a self-admitted spoiled rich boy, putting others' needs first. I took a bite of the sandwich and grinned at Charity. "This is definitely a new classic," I said. "Let's keep this on our menu rotation."

A dog yipped, so I glanced over toward the Barks section. Bristol was tossing a rubber bone to a spotted white mutt that had the big, docile head of a Great Pyrenees. She slipped her hand into her back pocket and retrieved her cell phone, then pressed it to her ear. She must've gotten a call.

I munched on my sandwich, soaking in the relaxing vibe of the cafe. Kylie and Milo had designed a playlist of folksy music that subtly piped through the speaker system. The leather-backed barstool was well cushioned and had a metal bar underneath so my shorter legs weren't left dangling. I stared at the blue-red flames of the fire and started to zone out.

"Macy."

Bristol's wobbly voice snapped me back to attention. She stood behind my chair, anxiously shifting on her feet.

I whirled to face her. "What's wrong?"

Her brown eyes were wide and disbelieving. "My uncle's awake."

13

Once Bristol told me her mom had already gone to work, I sprang into action. "Why don't you ask Milo if he could fill in for you? I'll let Bo know I'm taking you to the hospital," I instructed.

It was a calculated move to have Bristol ask Milo, because I had the sneaking suspicion that he'd been harboring a crush on my dark-eyed dog-sitter for a while now. Might as well capitalize on it now, since Charity wasn't the best at handling dogs and Bo was the most efficient at whipping up the specialty drinks. Surprisingly, Milo was pretty good with the dogs, although he hadn't owned any pets growing up.

"Okay," Bristol said, her eyes brimming. I wanted to ask if her uncle Clark had said anything, but she probably didn't even know yet.

Milo agreed to oversee the Barks section far more readily than I'd dared to hope, and Bo encouraged me to get Bristol to the hospital as soon as possible. I wished I had an extra car to give the poor girl, since she always seemed to be bumming rides off others. But even if she could afford to buy a junker, the insurance would be hard to cover because of her age.

Detective Hatcher stood outside the doorway to Clark's room, holding up a cautioning hand as we strode toward him. "Can't go in now, I'm afraid. He was talking a little—even answered some questions—but then he kind of drifted off, and the nurse told us we had to let him rest."

Bristol looked deflated. "My mom—did you let her know? She's at work. I have her number if you—"

Detective Hatcher interrupted. "I've already called and let her know the situation," he assured her. Gesturing to a white-haired woman in scrubs, he told Bristol, "You might want to ask her for more details."

Bristol hurried over to the woman, so I took the opportunity to follow up with the detective. "Did you get my text about Della being near the crash site, probably soon after the wreck? And are there any updates on that camera that was in the vase? Also, did you find Les Stevens?"

Detective Hatcher gave a half-smile. "Whoa, Nelly. Yes, I got your message, and I've been in touch with Della. As for that video camera, Les Stevens' prints were all over it, but there wasn't anything unexpected on it—just footage of when he was setting it up. And finally, no, we haven't been able to track Les down."

Bristol appeared to be deep in conversation with the nurse, so I plunged on. "So...you said Clark answered questions. Did you ask about the wreck? Did he see anything?"

Detective Hatcher gave me a long look. "Since your brother was with the DEA, I trust you know how to keep things quiet. And I'm only telling you this because it might link to the man Bristol described as attacking her—possibly the same one you've seen lurking around town. I want you to call me if he shows up again."

"Got it," I said.

The detective rubbed at the dark stubble on his chin. "Clark said something extraordinary—that someone was standing in the road on the day of the wreck. Even more crazy, he said the man had a grenade launcher. When I asked him for a description, he just said something about long blond hair. That was all I got from him before he dozed off."

A *grenade launcher*? How on earth had the blond man managed to get hold of *that*?

This did not bode well for Bristol's family. If that lunatic was able to get hold of a weapon that could take out an armored truck, he might return to the Goddard home, this time armed to the teeth.

Detective Hatcher seemed to read my thoughts. "I'm having an officer patrol the Goddards' street twice a day," he said. "From what our sources say, that blond one hasn't left the country yet."

"Thanks." I glanced at Bristol, who seemed to be winding up her chat. "Should I tell *her* that the man who attacked her might still be around?"

"That would be helpful, if you wouldn't mind—I need to get back to the station. Her mother's already been updated on the situation. Also, I'm counting on you and Bo to keep an eye on Bristol when she works at the cafe."

I didn't flinch as the detective's hazel eyes drilled into mine. "You didn't even have to ask," I said firmly.

He cracked a small smile. "I figured. I've heard a lot about you Hatfields, and you sure don't seem like the type to let anyone sneak up on ya."

I wasn't aware we had some kind of reputation. "You mean Bo and me?" I asked, confused. Sure, the detective knew about our involvement in bringing down a fencing ring a few months ago, but that didn't seem to be what he was referring to.

His smile widened. "No, ma'am. I'm talking about your aunt Athaleen. She was a force to be reckoned with, no doubt. My old boss, now retired, has several stories of things that happened before she took you two in." He raised an eyebrow. "You ought to go talk with him someday—his name's Mercer Priestly. He lives over in Fairlea now."

Before I could wipe the surprised look off my face, Bristol wheeled around and headed our way. Her light steps slowed the moment she glanced at me. "Everything okay?"

I gave a weak smile. "Things are okay with Clark, but I need to talk with you about something when we get back to the car." I turned back to the detective, trying to shake off the sudden realization that maybe Auntie A wasn't as transparent as I'd assumed. "Thanks for updating me. I'm sure you'll keep us posted if Clark wakes up."

Detective Hatcher gave me a knowing look. "Will do." He turned to Bristol. "Take care of yourself, young lady."

EVEN AFTER I warned Bristol that her attacker and his accomplice hadn't been apprehended, she still insisted on returning to work, so I drove her to the cafe and waited until she was safely inside. Then I promptly texted Bo and asked him to drop by my place after work so we could catch up.

As soon as I opened my back door, Coal crashed past me and careened into the garden. I let him frolic while I puttered around, checking my mailbox and rolling my emptied trash can back into the gardening shed. I finally gave a whistle, and Coal bounded toward me. Unable to put his brakes on in time, his rear end crashed into my shins.

"Coal, you've got to learn to curb your enthusiasm," I said, nonetheless enjoying the thrill of satisfaction that my dog loved spending time with me. I gave his huge, sleek forehead a pat. "Maybe we'll walk over and visit Stormy sometime. How'd you like that?"

Coal's tail thudded into my leg. I opened the door and followed him into the chilly house. My heating system had been acting up, so that was something else I'd have to talk with Bo about tonight.

Rummaging through my freezer, I found a microwaveable container of barbeque pork, which would work great for our meal since I still had leftover hamburger buns. I could whip up some of Auntie A's coleslaw to go with our sandwiches and open a fresh bag of Bo's favorite salt and vinegar chips, which I always kept on hand for him.

I felt unusually keyed up, as if I needed to get some exercise. Trying to pinpoint the cause of my angst, I rough-chopped half a head of cabbage to throw in the food processor. I was worried about Bristol, that was it. Not to mention Della and Ethan. Sure, the cops were doing a little patrolling, but would that be enough to ward off the guys who'd broken in last time?

My phone rang. Coal jumped up from his pillow and stared at it, giving the hilarious impression that he was about to head over and pick it up. "Thanks, boy," I said, laughing as I wiped my hands on my apron. "But I'll get that."

I picked up the phone, surprised to see who was calling. Sheldia Powers, the enthusiastic librarian.

"Macy, I'm glad I caught you. I'm sure you're busy with the cafe."

"Today's actually my day off," I said. "But yes, it's been pretty busy this month."

"I can imagine." Sheldia paused, and I sensed the small talk was over. "Listen, I was wondering...the Bookmobile visits the low income assisted living apartments once a month. I think it would be fantastic if we could take some tamer shelter dogs along on those visits, allowing the residents to bond with the animals."

It was a great idea, but an endeavor like that would likely be fraught with red tape. "Sounds good, but you'll need to contact the shelter director, Summer, and ask her about it," I said. "She's the one who works with the dog half of Barks & Beans, and I know she'd be much more knowledgeable about what they can do with the shelter dogs."

"Oh, sure." The silence that followed grew a little awkward.

Coal trotted over and pressed against my leg, angling for a pet. I rubbed behind his ear. "Uh, well, thanks for calling, but I need to get going on supper," I said.

"Okay." She still sounded hesitant, so I was forced to prod her on a bit.

"Was there anything else?" I asked.

"Were you all participating in the Girl's Day Out?" she asked.

"Barks & Beans, do you mean? Yes, we were. I hope you can drop in."

"I'll do that," she said. The faint strains of canned Christmas music played in the background, and I suspected she was still at the library. "Okay, thanks, Macy." She abruptly hung up.

Coal shot me a look as I returned the phone to the counter. "She's a bit unusual," I said.

"Who is?" Bo was standing in the doorway.

I whirled around. "How'd you get in so quietly?"

He grinned. "Drug Enforcement Agency, sis. I don't think I've explained how heavily we're trained, but let's just say I have some skills."

That fact was never in doubt. It was a given that my brother always carried his Glock in a holster somewhere on his person, and he was faithful to practice at the shooting range in his downtime. Plus, he had a key to my place, which had come in handy more than once.

"So who were you saying is unusual?" he continued, kicking his tan loafers off on the rubber mat just inside the door.

"Sheldia Powers." I flipped on the food processor, then scooped out the contents into a bowl before adding mayo.

Bo leaned against the counter. "What's Sheldia up to?"

I laid out Sheldia's Bookmobile idea for him. "But I had the weirdest feeling she wanted to talk about something else," I added, using my pinkie to take a small taste of the slaw and see if I used the right amount of vinegar.

Bo grabbed a spoon and took a small bite. "Maybe a little more salt, but it's close to Auntie A's," he said. "So what else would she want? Surely you're not still thinking she had something to do with the truck heist?"

"Probably not. Maybe she just wanted to ask about you. I'm convinced she still carries a torch for you. She could've been planning to ask me if you're dating, but instead got embarrassed and hung up."

Bo colored a bit under his freckles, and it was adorable. It wasn't often that I was able to fluster my rugged, stoic big brother. He grabbed the container of barbeque and deftly changed the subject. "I don't know about you, but I'm starving. I'm throwing this in the microwave."

ONCE WE'D SETTLED at the table and had a little food in our stomachs, I filled Bo in on what Clark had said about a grenade launcher.

"It seems so far-fetched, like something he recalled from a thriller movie, not from real life," I said. "I mean, who on earth has grenade launchers around here?"

Bo chewed thoughtfully on his bite of barbeque sandwich, then wiped his mouth. "Is it really so unbelievable, though? I mean, if I were going to take out an armored truck, that'd be one surefire way to go about it. Maybe this foreign guy and his partner have some connections around here—in fact, maybe his partner is even from this area."

"Maybe." I had an idea. "You should ask your friend Titan if he can dig up any info on them."

Titan McCoy was an FBI agent who had not only helped us tie up loose ends with the fencing ring, but he'd also kept us informed as to the whereabouts of Leo Moreau, a particularly vengeful arms dealer who had targeted my brother more than once. Although Leo had made a frightening personal call to my cell phone a few months ago, as far as the FBI and DEA knew, he was still living out of the country.

The fact that Titan's last name was McCoy never failed to tickle my Hatfield funny bone, although I knew the original feud between those families was no laughing matter.

"Sure. I'll need their names—"

"Detective Hatcher has them. He didn't tell me, and he didn't tell me what country that blond guy was from, either." I ate a chip and washed it down with a gulp of water. "Since Clark pointed a finger at the blond man, he must not have been working *with* them on the heist, as I'd feared."

"Right." Bo glanced at Coal, who was politely sitting at the edge of the dining room rug, his eyes half-shut. "Your dog is more behaved around food than my cat. That just seems backward."

I grinned. "You know he's watching our every move under those eyelids, just hoping someone will crack and throw him a scrap." I stood and stretched.

Coal immediately got to his feet. I padded over and grabbed a dog treat from the jar and handed it to him. As I washed my hands, I said, "Detective Hatcher seems to think Bristol and her family might still be in danger."

"And what about Clark?" Bo asked. "If he's awake and spouting information, someone might target him, too. I know Charlie Hatcher's a great guy, but he can't have his men running protective duty all the time. I'll get those names for Titan, so he can check them out."

"Thanks." I sat back down and rested my chin on my hands. "So...if you're not interested in Sheldia, who *would* you be interested in?"

"Wouldn't you like to know," Bo said, shooting me a mischievous smile.

14

My phone alarm blasted the loud strains of a techno rendition of "We Wish you a Merry Christmas." I swiped toward my bedside table in an attempt to snooze the alarm, but instead managed to knock my phone onto the wood floor. Sighing, I sat up, leaned over, and flipped the screen upward. I was happy to see it was still intact. I turned the alarm off altogether. I might as well get up, since I needed to be at work in about twenty minutes.

Coal hadn't even raised his head during all my bedside hubbub, but once I slid out of the warm covers, he stretched and lumbered to my side, anxious for a petting. In the months I'd owned him, his doggie pillow had inched closer and closer until he'd positioned it at the foot of my bed. At first I thought he'd chosen that area so he'd have lots of room to sprawl out, but I'd recently realized his preference was far more calculated than that. His pillow was directly in line with my bedroom door, because he intended to be the first line of defense if an intruder walked in.

It was honestly the most endearing thing ever.

I walked him downstairs and fed him before whipping together some particularly lackluster oatmeal for myself. I'd decided to eat healthy in an attempt to lose the pounds that had crept up on me around Thanksgiving. As I tried to chew the steel cut oats, wondering if anyone on earth actually enjoyed their gravelly texture, I checked my email. As usual, there was nothing but junk messages. My text box was empty.

I had to admit I sort of missed the early days of marriage when Jake would head out to work before I did. He'd always send a text telling me to have a great day, and he'd include a compliment, like *I love the feel of your hair*, or *You smell like vanilla and caramel and I can't wait to come home to you.*

Chomping down on a tooth-breaker piece of oat, I grimaced and spat it into a napkin. Those morning texts had stopped about two years into our marriage...was that when Jake started cheating, I wondered?

It wasn't worth thinking about, I told myself for the hundredth time.

I let Coal out into the garden, then ran upstairs since I was already running a little late. I located a pair of black jeans and a tomato red sweater that complemented rather than competed with the red in my hair. By the time I'd applied some light powder and mascara, I knew I had to skedaddle over to the cafe so I'd get there in time to meet Summer and get the shelter dog scoop o' the day.

Coal came in the moment I whistled for him, so I grabbed my keys and gave him a hurried goodbye. I headed down my hallway and unlocked the connecting door into the cafe. I didn't mind using it this time of day, when there weren't any customers around.

Bo was already busy behind the counter, but he glanced over as I walked in. "You sleep okay, sis?"

I patted at my wavy hair, which had been impossible to whip into shape. "Sure, why? Do I look weird?"

Before he had the chance to answer, Summer came in the cafe door with three dogs prancing alongside her. I immediately fixated on a gorgeous, pale caramel-colored dog that had to be a purebred Doodle of some kind.

"Where'd you get that one?" I asked.

She grinned. "Interesting you should ask...are you looking for another dog, Macy? This one's a Labradoodle, and she has a rather interesting backstory."

The soft-looking Doodle trotted out on its leash, anxious to sniff me. I couldn't look away from its little brown teddy bear eyes.

Summer continued. "Her owners paid a lot to get her, then they had her spayed, like their contract demanded. But when they took her to training school, she was too interested in the other dogs to pay attention to commands. By the time the family realized they couldn't handle her, the return clause in their contract had expired. They had to move, so they brought her to the shelter."

"And now you brought her for a visit to Barks & Beans." I leaned in to scratch under her chin. "What's her name?"

"Well...they'd named her Waffles," Summer said. "She had the habit of grabbing their kids' waffles when no one was looking."

"Aw, Waffles." I looked into the dog's sad eyes. "Sounds like you had to leave a lot behind."

Summer led the dogs into the petting section and unleashed them. "Now before you get all misty-eyed, I'm going to tell you the rest of the story. The family dropped this wild child with me two nights ago, since I wasn't able to check her into the shelter until morning. Waffles proceeded to terrorize my cats, turn my trash can inside out, relieve herself on my carpet—several times—then howl from the moment I put her into her crate until the middle of the night." She shook her head. "I can't even tell you how she's going to behave for you today—*if* she's going to behave at all. But she is a purebred dog, so I figured she'd have a good chance of getting adopted."

"She's so adorable."

Summer gave me an exasperated look. "Well, beauty only goes so far, Macy."

Bo's voice surprised me. "Ain't that the truth." He was leaning against the divider wall, a smile playing at his lips.

Summer's head immediately snapped up. Try as she might, she couldn't hide the way her gaze slid over his hair, eyes, and beard, then rested for a split second on his muscles.

Bo was still staring at Waffles as if unaware of his magnetism. "She seems calm enough now," he remarked.

Sure enough, Waffles had chosen a chew toy and sedately settled on a mat. She turned a rather pointed gaze our way, as if dismayed at the way her good name had been maligned.

Bo looked at Summer. "Speaking of calm, do you have any idea when Stormy will start settling down? I mean, kittens *do* settle down, right?"

It didn't take long for Waffles to live down to Summer's low expectations. After spending one blissful hour playing contentedly with the ball, she became aware that people were coming into the cafe—*lots* of people. She began yipping and jumping higher than the divider wall, trying to get the cafe customers' attention. If there were an award for the doggie high jump, she would've earned it.

I finally had to throw in the towel when the goofy dog managed to launch herself from a foam block onto the wooden ledge topping the divider wall. I shot over, trying to clip the leash onto her collar, but it was too late. She'd already taken a nosedive onto the cafe floor. Unfazed, she immediately scrambled to her feet and dashed toward one man's chicken croissant.

The bewildered man reached out to slide his sandwich back. Just before Waffles managed to snag it, Bo placed a firm hand on her collar so she had to come to a screeching halt. Waffles gave a plaintive yelp, but I knew it was in vain.

My brother turned to me. The look on his face was impossible to misunderstand. He had made up his mind, and there was nothing on earth that would deter him. "She's going back to the shelter," he said.

When Bo gave a command like that, I knew better than to cross him. Besides, no matter how cute Waffles was, she was indeed the living terror Summer had made her out to be.

"I'll take her," I volunteered. Glancing over, I saw that Jimmy had already left for lunch break and that Kylie was swamped with serving customers. "Just hang on a few minutes —I'll see if Bristol can fill in for me. I'll keep Waffles outside in the run until then."

Bo nodded, releasing the now-leashed dog. His blue eyes softened. "Thanks—and sorry, sis. She is a cute dog, but she's not a great fit for Barks & Beans."

"You've got that right." I walked the panting dog back to the Barks section. Since the other two dogs were enjoying pets from customers, I grabbed my coat before leading Waffles out the side door and into the fenced dog run.

She gazed up at me with a look that seemed to ask what she had done wrong.

"Just about everything," I muttered, gripping the leash handle so she couldn't jump the fence. I pulled out my phone and called Bristol, who said her mom was just heading to the grocery store, so she'd drop her off at the cafe so she could fill in for me.

"I'm glad you called," Bristol said. "I've been sitting around, playing chess with Ethan, and he beats me every time."

A loud victory whoop sounded in the background. Ethan was obviously proud of his achievement.

"See what I mean?" Bristol asked. "Anyway, I'll be over soon."

I hung up and looked at Waffles, who had sunk to the ground in a dejected heap. "Aren't you pitiful," I said, looking into those world-weary eyes. "I sure hope you can straighten up somehow, doggie." But something told me Waffles was in an unmanageable class by herself.

I WATCHED over the fence until I saw Della's small car pull up in front of the cafe. I reeled the leash in tighter before walking Waffles back into the petting section. For one split second, I thought she'd calmed down and was going to trot along happily by my side, but I was quickly proved wrong. She started lunging and jumping toward the other dogs—and the customers. I gripped the leash and rushed out the front door and onto the sidewalk, where I nearly collided with a kind-looking older man who was about to head into Barks & Beans.

"Sorry—so sorry, sir," I breathed, avoiding eye contact as I made a beeline for Della's car. Bristol was already standing on the sidewalk. She took a step backward when she saw our frantic approach.

"Sorry!" I shouted, pulling the leash as tight as I could. Waffles plunked onto the ground in front of Bristol, unwilling to back up toward me.

Bristol gave a knowing nod. "Got a bad seed today, eh?"

"I guess so." I glared at the wayward dog, but she was staring across the street at nothing in particular. "I'm going to load her up and take her to the shelter. It shouldn't take long to drop her off. I'm sorry to have to ask you to fill in."

Bristol waved her hand. Her nails were painted bright turquoise and had black tips. "Don't rush. Honestly, I don't mind hanging around the rest of the day, if you want."

Given the way my day had gone thus far, it was a tempting offer. "I'll let you know. Thanks again." I leaned down to wave at Della, who appeared to be deep in a phone conversation. She held up a finger, as if she wanted to say something to me, so I patiently stood near Waffles as Bristol headed inside.

A mother and daughter duo stepped out of a nearby bistro and stopped to exclaim over my curly-haired doggie burden.

"Isn't she *sweet?*" The teen leaned down and made kissy noises.

"Where do you have her trimmed?" The mother batted her long false eyelashes at me, genuinely interested.

"Uh—she's a shelter dog, actually. She just visited Barks & Beans for part of the day." What a euphemism, as if Waffles had been out on the town and decided to drop in on her lunch break.

The woman pressed her hand to her chest. "I had no idea they had purebred dogs in there." She hitched her designer bag a little higher on her shoulder and gestured to her daughter. "Burberry here has been *dying* for a new puppy, but honestly I don't know if I have the stamina for one, you know?"

I was about to point out that Burberry was definitely old enough to care for a pet on her own—after all, that's what I'd done all my life—but Della knocked on the passenger window.

"Sorry, I have to go." I glanced at Burberry, who was not-so-politely picking at a piece of food stuck in her teeth. I gave her what I hoped was a winning smile. "I hope you'll visit the cafe sometime. My brother and I own it." I was rewarded with a bored stare.

The mother gave me a curious look, like she wasn't sure what to make of a working woman. Waffles, who had somehow managed to sit quietly during the entire exchange, suddenly jumped to her feet and gave a booming bark, which caused both her ardent admirers to scurry along.

"Way to go," I whispered, nudging the dog closer to Della's car.

Della had cranked down her window, and she was leaning across the driver's seat, making urgent motions to me. I rushed closer and leaned down. "What's going on?"

The dark-haired woman looked stunned. "Les got shot! And something's up—he wants me to meet him, but he said not to call the cops. He's waiting in some out-of-the-way trailer." She seemed a bit breathless. "Macy, I can't go alone, because I don't really trust him, but he insinuated it had something to do with my brother." She glanced at the dog. "Could you get away and come with me? I know it's last-minute, but I just don't know who else to ask."

I looked down at Waffles, who had her ears pricked, as if personally considering Della's offer.

I tried to understand. "I don't know. I mean, I guess I could, but I'll need to drop the dog off at the shelter. Did Les say what happened?"

Della unlocked her doors. "There's no time to explain. Just put the dog in the back; we'll drop her off on the way home."

I had a moment's hesitation. What if Della was the thief and, by default, Christian's murderer? What if she was working with the grenade launcher men and they'd decided I was getting too close somehow?

Taking a good look at her fearful, concerned face, I felt confident that she wasn't lying. She was a fellow church member and single mom who'd been put a situation where she needed some backup, that was all.

I opened the back door, pushing Waffles in before plopping down beside her.

"Hit it," I said.

15

As DELLA's car putted along, trying to pick up speed, she explained things a little more. "When Les called, at first he said he wanted me to meet him to discuss Clark's vacation time and insurance. I said I could drop by Stevens Security later on this afternoon. Les said no, he wanted me to meet him somewhere private. I realized it might be a sneaky way of getting me alone. I never have trusted him."

"Me either." I stretched my legs as Waffles moved toward the opposite side of the seat and shoved her nose through the open window crack. She gulped at the fresh air as it rushed by.

"Anyway, he said he was going to be at his trailer for a while. He gave me the address—it's just off Glen Bridge Road. He wanted me to come over around five. I was about to refuse, but then something happened."

"Which is why we're rushing over to the trailer now," I finished, shoving back thick locks of hair that kept blowing into my mouth and eyes.

"Exactly," she said, placing her free hand on the wheel as if to steady her frayed nerves. "While he was talking to me, someone drove up. He said someone was meeting him so he had to go. But before he could hang up, I heard this"—her voice wavered—"this popping sound. Like fireworks, several of them. Then next thing I know, Les says he was shot in his stomach, and to come quick. Only he said not to call the cops."

"But I don't get it," I said, trying to put the pieces together. "Why wouldn't he want the cops?"

"I don't know," Della said, righting the wheel after a sharp curve. "But I called emergency services right after I hung up and gave them the address. I mean, the man could be dying for all I know."

"That was wise," I said.

"Let's hope they get there first," she said. "I just don't get why he was so hush-hush."

I didn't want to float the theory that perhaps Les was involved in the truck heist—and maybe he'd gone in with someone like Della's own brother.

In a sudden moment of friendliness, Waffles sank back onto the seat and nuzzled against my side. I gave her head a pat. When she wasn't being completely insane, the dog was sweet, I had to admit.

Della slowed as we approached the town of Ronceverte. I plugged the house number into the maps app on my phone, but when we turned off on the dirt road that supposedly led to the place, we both wondered if Les had given the wrong address.

There *was* a trailer at the end of the short lane, but it wasn't a trailer anyone would live in. It was blown-out—quite literally—complete with scorch marks up the sides. Windows had been boarded over, and the also-blackened roof was caving in on one side.

The sad trailer looked like a casualty of a meth lab fire.

Not one emergency vehicle had arrived. After a little discussion, we both decided we couldn't wait around for EMS, despite how hazardous the place looked. As I opened the door, Waffles unfortunately jumped across the seat and plunged outside. I hadn't even clipped her leash on yet.

"Shoot!" I shouted, scrambling to catch up to the dog, who had already run up on the rickety front porch and was sniffing at the metal screen door, which ironically had no screen.

I pounded up the stairs and got the leash on Waffles, hoping I hadn't made too much racket in the process. If the shooter had decided to stay behind for some reason...I tried to swallow my nervousness. Maybe it wouldn't hurt to have a dog along for this dangerous adventure, even if she was dumber than dirt.

Della jogged off to the side of the trailer, where the back end of a blue car was visible. "It's Les'," Della mouthed, circling back toward the porch.

She reached into her outer purse pocket. I assumed she was digging for her phone, but she extracted a slim purple pistol instead. It took me a moment to register that it was a real gun, as opposed to some kind of child's toy.

Guns were nothing new to me—after all, my brother had bought me a .22 rifle when I'd turned sixteen, and he'd made sure to take me to the shooting range many times. I wondered if Della had much experience with hers, but the moment I saw her wrap her other hand around the grip, her finger lying flat above the trigger guard so as not to inadvertently fire, I felt a surge of confidence. Della was no gun newbie. She knew exactly what she was doing.

She jerked her head to the left, indicating that I should step aside and let her go first. Waffles, who oddly hadn't barked once, nearly tripped me as I moved out of Della's way. I pulled the leash tight, but it wasn't necessary. The frisky Labradoodle's latest trick was sticking so close that I could barely put one foot in front of the other.

I was sure this dog was perfect for *someone*, but definitely not for me. I missed my big lug of a Dane, now more than ever. He would instinctively know I wanted him to sit tight, without my even asking him. We were on the same wavelength and knew how to work as a unit.

As Della pulled the screen door open, it gave a loud creak. I felt another rush of apprehension. Where were the EMT workers, anyway? We should've called the cops, no matter what Les said.

Della twisted the worn front knob and the door opened. Either the shooters hadn't bothered to lock it, or they were still inside.

Della's gun was at the ready as she pushed past the door into the trailer. The smell of mildew hit me square in the face. Unable to think of any better options for Waffles, who was about to yank the leash from my hands anyway, I let her lead me onto the threadbare carpet just inside the door. I hesitated a moment so my eyes could adjust to the shifting lighting, which was filtering through gaps in the ceiling. The windows were boarded over and didn't allow daylight in.

"Over here!" Della's shout was loud and urgent, so she must be reasonably sure no one had stayed behind.

Following Della's voice, Waffles took off down the hallway. I clambered along, trying to keep up with her. She made a sharp left into the first bedroom. I pulled her leash tighter as I caught up and peered into the room.

Della had sunk to the ground near a battered futon where Les' body was sprawled out. She had her finger on his neck, checking for a pulse.

Blood seeped from a wound in his lower chest, staining both the worn blue cushion and the tufts of stuffing popping out of it. It was clear from the white look of Les' lips and face that if he wasn't dead yet, he unfortunately would be soon.

"What can we do?" I pulled Waffles up close to my side so she wouldn't investigate the blood.

"I'm not sure." Della gave up checking for a pulse and edged closer to Les' face. Giving his pale cheek a small slap, she said, "Les, it's me, Della. Les?"

The man gasped and opened his eyes, but they stared straight ahead as if he were unable to focus. "Della?" he croaked out.

"Yes, it's me." She patted at his hand. "What happened?"

His voice sounded thick, as if filled with phlegm. "It's...not the money," he said.

"What?" Della leaned in. "The truck money, you mean?"

He gave a nearly imperceptible nod. "They want..." He coughed, sending a spray of blood onto Della's white shirt.

I gagged. I wasn't good with blood. Like some kind of vampire, it always made my sense of smell sharpen, and right now, the hot, rusty scent of blood mingled with the stench of rotting weeds that had infiltrated the trailer. The resulting cloying aroma seemed to drape over me like a thick net.

My hands started tingling and my ears seemed to fill, making my head heavy. Knowing I was heading straight for a regular old-fashioned faint, I sank to the floor and put my head between my knees. In a stunning twist of compassion, Waffles trotted to my side, nudging at my hair. Or maybe she was just trying to eat it.

Les said something else, but I couldn't make it out. I did hear Della say, "Oh, no," and then some weird stomping sound seemed to echo in my head.

Della's voice got closer. "They're here," she said. "Hang on."

I FELT like an idiot as a handsome EMT rolled up a stretcher and helped me ease onto it. "I'm fine, really," I said. "It was just a dizzy spell, that's all."

Della stood nearby, Waffles' leash in hand. Her gun was nowhere in sight, so I assumed she'd slipped it back in her purse the moment emergency services had pulled up. "Just let them take you out on the stretcher, Macy," she said. "You've been kind of out of it."

The "ride" on the stretcher was far from relaxing, so by the time they got me down the steps, I was fully alert. I shrugged out of my coat so they could slide the blood pressure cuff up my arm.

Motioning Della over, I asked, "Did Les make it?"

She shook her head. "He was too far gone. He never told me who shot him, either."

"Blood pressure's fine," the man said, smiling at me. His blond hair, beard, and arm tattoo made him look some kind of Norse god. "You're okay to get up now, if you feel like it." He handed me a water bottle.

I gave him a cursory nod. Blonds were not on my dating agenda, for now and for always, thanks to Jake. And redheads reminded me too much of my brother, handsome though they were. Nope, it was dark haired men from here on out, if and when I started dating in earnest. Which might be never.

I slid off the stretcher none too gracefully, nearly stepping on Waffles' paw. Not one to pass up the opportunity to cause a little chaos, Waffles backed up and proceeded to take a flying leap...right onto the stretcher.

One thing was certain, that dog could jump.

Della and I managed to wrangle Waffles back to the ground. We led her directly over to Della's car, where a police officer waited, presumably to talk with us.

"You get in with the dog and I'll talk with him," Della instructed, tossing her keys to me.

Waffles climbed into the back seat and I reluctantly sat next to her. The windows were still cracked from when we'd arrived, so I could overhear Della's report. After sharing about Les' phone call and our drive over, she began to repeat what Les had said with his dying breaths.

"He said it wasn't about the money. I assumed he was talking about the money that went missing from one of his armored security trucks a little over a week ago."

The officer nodded. He was definitely aware of the truck crash, as was the entire Lewisburg community. "Anything else?"

"Just one thing at the very end," she said.

I perked up. This must've been what Les had said when the rushing in my head had drowned out other sounds.

"He said something I couldn't make out, except for the word 'diamonds.' Then his eyes..." She took a couple of deep breaths, and her voice shook when she spoke. "I don't know how to explain it, except that the light went out of them. He died right there, right next to me."

My mind went into overdrive. *Diamonds?* Les had segued from talking about the heist money to talking about diamonds. That couldn't be a coincidence.

The officer wrapped things up, and Della got into the car. I asked her to run me by the animal shelter and then drop me at home, if she didn't mind. She nodded mutely. She'd had more than one shock recently, and watching a man die right in front of her had only made things worse. I didn't make any chitchat along the way; instead, I simply petted Waffles in hopes she would stay still.

We arrived at the shelter, and I ran Waffles inside. Summer was full of profuse apologies when I handed her the leash and explained why I was bringing the dog back, but I brushed them aside. "It's not your fault. I think Waffles is really too energetic to be an indoor dog," I said. "Maybe she needs a place with lots of room to run, like a farm."

Summer nodded, setting her ponytail bobbing. "Good idea. I'll keep that in mind. I actually have a possible foster family lined up for her. They're coming in to meet her tomorrow. I think they have some yard space."

I glanced at the Labradoodle, who gazed up at me from her seated position as if she was living her best life. I supposed that today, she had been.

"Good luck with the meeting," I said, and I meant it. Waffles needed a loving home just as badly as any other abandoned dog. Coal himself had been in this very shelter once, not very long ago, and look what a great pet he'd turned out to be.

Then again, Coal had extensive dog training under his belt. I couldn't imagine how crazy it would be to live with a dog the size of a Great Dane who had no boundaries and didn't obey at all.

I shook off my negative thoughts and told Summer goodbye. As I walked out to Della's car, I felt torn as to whether I should bring up Les' last words or not.

Della saved me the trouble of deciding. Once I sat down in the passenger seat, she turned to me. "Les said something about diamonds, but there's been no mention of them in relation to what was stolen in the truck heist. Don't you think that's odd?"

I gave a nod. "Yes, I definitely do."

Now we had to ask ourselves who'd been lying about the contents of the truck. Les? Or maybe the banker who'd loaded the goods?

Or even...I didn't want to go there in my mind, but hadn't it been Detective Hatcher who'd told reporters that only $500,000 in cash had gone missing? Was it possible he'd gone in with Les to cover up the fact that diamonds were hidden on that truck? Maybe they'd been searching for them together.

What if he'd been working with the blond man and his cohort, and had been lying to me about them?

If I'd been feeding information to the wrong person, I'd feel like a fool. But Charlie Hatcher was a police detective, so surely he should be trustworthy, right?

I needed to talk to Bo. He could tell me if Detective Hatcher had ever shared the blond man's name or found out who Joe Watkins really was. If the blond was really from another country, we might need some help from Bo's DEA or FBI friends. Maybe it was time for my brother to call in the reinforcements.

16

When I got home, I changed into comfier clothes, then gave Coal a thorough and very appreciative petting. More than ever, I was grateful for my huge, loving, and mostly couch-potato dog.

After boiling water and steeping my bag of Earl Gray, I added liberal cream and sugar. I took a long, comforting sip before calling Bristol to make sure she was okay with finishing out my shift.

I had no intention of informing her that her mom and I had just witnessed the drawn-out death of Les Stevens. I'd leave that up to Della's discretion. Although Auntie A had raised us with our eyes wide open, keeping us abreast of any news that happened in town, I knew not all moms shared that approach.

Bristol was chipper when she answered and said the remaining two dogs had behaved admirably. In fact, one customer had bonded with the smaller one and planned to adopt him on Monday. She was more than happy to fill in the remainder of the day.

Ready for a change of pace, I texted Bo and asked if Coal

and I could join him on his evening run—with the caveat that it would be more like a walk. He readily agreed, texting back that the cafe had been busy, which was what we'd expect on a Saturday in December.

It was hard to believe our little doggie cafe was already in the black—thanks largely to Bo's contribution of personally covering the renovation and outfitting of the place. He told me he'd socked away plenty of liquid assets when he'd retired early from his job at Coffee Mass, but I got the feeling I hadn't even seen the tip of the iceberg as far as what he'd saved up.

It was funny to me that Bo never hobnobbed with the town's wealthy clique—I mean, he had the money, and if you slapped a tux on him, he'd look like James Bond. But he rarely visited the Greenbrier, he wasn't into golfing, and he didn't spring for incredibly expensive restaurants or clothing.

Taking my last swig of Earl Gray, I curled up on the couch and flipped on a baking show. Coal tentatively placed a paw next to my foot, "asking" if he could join me.

"Go ahead," I said, feeling magnanimous.

He proceeded to back onto a couch cushion, sitting on his posterior just like a human. He braced his front paws on the floor, so he appeared to be watching TV.

Every time he got into this position, I burst out laughing. This time was no exception.

He cocked his head at me, demanding an explanation of my response to what he deemed normal behavior.

I rubbed his head. "Sorry, my dapper friend. You're just too cute for your own good, and I love ya."

COAL GAVE A SINGLE DEEP BARK, rousing me from my nap. I must've been out for a while, because Bo was giving his recognizable secret knock on my back door. "I am a Rock" by Simon & Garfunkel was one of his favorite throwback songs, and now the tune was being rapped out lickety-split.

"Coming!" I shouted, wondering why my brother hadn't just let himself in like he did last time. I threw the door open and instantly wished I'd donned something other than yoga pants and an oversized, ratty-edged Tootsie Roll sweatshirt I'd had since high school.

It turned out that my brother hadn't come alone. In fact, it turned out that Titan McCoy was standing right in front of me.

The tall hulk of a man, whose first name could not have been more apt, gave me the fastest once-over I'd ever been privy to. The slightest hint of a grin crossed his lips, but he quickly got it in check. "Hi there. Sorry to drop in unannounced, but I was in town, talking with Detective Hatcher. I'm only in for tonight. Bo said—"

Bo interrupted, obviously anxious to get going since the sun was already setting. "I told him to come walking with us. Work slowed down, so I asked Jimmy to close up for me." Bo stretched his calves, then jogged down into the garden and started doing lunges.

Titan didn't seem overly anxious to get walking. He wasn't dressed in sports gear, like Bo—instead, he wore jeans and a charcoal sweater. I glanced at his feet, glad to see he wore sturdy hiking boots.

"Okay, hang on." Although I hadn't planned on seeing Titan, this was the perfect opportunity to catch both men up on the tragic events of the day. "Let me grab Coal."

Coal was exuberant as I clicked the leash onto his high quality leather collar, a memento from his days with his previous owner. Trotting along beside me, he looked every inch a show dog, from his pricked ears to his muscular haunches.

As we opened my back gate and stepped onto the sidewalk,

Bo jogged ahead of us by a few paces. "Go ahead and talk; I'll stay within earshot," he said.

Coal walked behind Bo, and Titan and I pulled up the rear.

"I have some news," I announced.

"About Les Stevens' death?" Titan asked.

I shot him an irritated look. "You already know about that?"

Once again, that partial grin threatened to overtake his face. "Detective Hatcher filled me in. And I told Bo on the way over. Sorry, Tootsie."

Flames of embarrassment licked at my cheeks as he referenced my shabby sweatshirt. I turned away from him, motioning wildly to one of the more stately houses in town. "Isn't this a great place?" I asked.

Bo slowed and turned, forcing us to come to a near-halt. His blue eyes met my own. "Now, sis, don't get mad because we scooped you. I thought you wanted Titan to check up on the strangers who've been stalking Bristol, so he did." Without waiting for my response, Bo picked up his pace and started jogging again.

I could feel Titan staring, so I looked up at him. In the sunset's warm rays, I got a good look at his eye color, which I hadn't paid attention to last time we'd met. It was a kind of indescribable shade of light brown that was shot through with gold.

Coal tugged on the leash and started following Bo again, so Titan and I fell into step behind him.

Titan spoke quietly, his voice surprisingly gentle for such a big man. "First, that house you pointed out *is* fantastic. You really don't see pillars like that anymore. Also, I'm sorry for picking on you about the shirt. I happened to love Tootsie Rolls as a kid, so I couldn't resist."

I cleared my throat, hoping the color in my face was dying down. It wasn't every day a girl got an apology from an FBI agent. "No problem. Did Detective Hatcher mention that Les said something about diamonds?"

Titan nodded. "I've put in a call to check for diamonds that went missing recently—either in the U.S. or internationally. Should hear back soon from my intel guy."

We picked up the pace as we approached a small hill. I didn't mind that Coal was practically pulling me along. I could probably sit on his back like a horse, and he wouldn't care.

I turned to Titan. "So...you trust Detective Hatcher, right?"

He gave me a curious look. "Sure, his background checks out. Why, do you have some reason to suspect he's involved in this?"

"I just got to thinking, what if he knew about the missing diamonds right off, and he was working with Les or someone to hide that they were stolen?"

Titan chuckled. "You have a great imagination, Macy. But no, the detective has been working with us all along to track down the missing stash. I'm sure he was as unaware of any diamonds as we were."

Bo topped the hill and turned. He was sweating, but other than that, didn't seem too exhausted. It seemed I hadn't gotten my brother's exercise genetics, because I was utterly pooped.

"Can we just rest a minute?" I asked, knowing I sounded lame.

Bo wiped his forehead. "How about I keep running the loop and I'll meet you two at my place? I know Stormy would love to see Coal." He grinned.

"That'll be fine," Titan said, before I could get a word in edgewise.

Wait—was my brother trying to set me up? Create some alone time with his good friend Titan?

"Okay, see ya," Bo said, breaking into a run down the street.

Good grief. I leaned against a stone wall, suddenly unsure

what to talk about. "Did you all find out anything else about Les Stevens? Like who he might've been connected with?"

"We're going over the records from Stevens Security now, but so far, they look clean. Whatever he was doing must've been on his own time."

I really needed a water bottle and wished I would've thought to pack one. "How about we head back to Bo's?" I suggested. Darkness had already started falling.

"Sure." As we started walking, Titan said, "Do you miss South Carolina? Bo said you moved back from there."

Bo must not have told Titan the whole story. "No, I don't miss it at all. My job with the DMV was going nowhere, and my husband cheated and left me."

"Oh, I'm sorry," Titan said. "I didn't mean to pry."

"No worries. I'm really glad to be home again, and I honestly don't mind sharing about the divorce. After all, it wasn't my fault." I looked up at him. "What about you? Are you from West Virginia originally? You don't seem to have any kind of accent."

He nodded. "I'm from the Wheeling area."

"So you're a Yankee," I joked.

He gave me a mock salute. "I still drink my tea sweet, though."

"Then you're a regular enigma." Street lights flickered on around us, lending their charming air to the evening. Titan was an enigma in more ways than one—I was dying to ask if he was married. He didn't wear a wedding band, but that might be because of his job.

The silence stretched on a bit, with only the sound of Coal's panting and the occasional passing vehicle to break it up.

"I'm divorced, too," Titan suddenly volunteered. His posture relaxed a little, like he was relieved to get that out in the open, but he didn't explain things further.

"Oh," I said. We were nearly to Bo's house, which already had the porch light burning. So my brother had made it back before we did. He surely didn't mess around when it came to keeping fit.

Titan seemed to want to say something, but must've thought better of it. We followed Coal up the steps, where he took a moment to lap up the water Bo had set out in a bowl for him.

Bo opened the door, rubbing at his head with a towel.

"Wait—did you *shower* already?" I asked.

He nodded. "Yeah, why? I take fast showers, sis. Come on in and have something to drink."

Coal took his last slurp and hurried inside. He was eager to see his kitten "friend."

True to form, Stormy flounced toward us, unfazed by the huge dog staring straight at her. Purring, she padded right past Coal and began weaving around my legs.

I picked up the little multicolored ball of fluff. "You silly kitty." She rolled over in my palms, squirming with delight. "She's so cute, Bo."

Bo dropped ice cubes in a couple of glasses of sweet tea. "Don't let her fool you. She puked in one of my shoes last night."

Titan took his glass of tea and sat down on one of the stools next to Bo's kitchen island. "Thanks, man." He scrolled around on his phone, oblivious to Stormy's adorable antics.

Coal, however, was not. He watched the kitten's every move. I still had a few misgivings about the two animals together. I trusted Coal, sure, but with a bite-sized kitty? So far, he'd stayed well away from her and tried to mind his own business. But what if she took to climbing on him or scratching him?

Bo brought me a glass, and I handed Stormy off to him. I

grinned as my tough brother brought the soft kitten to his cheek for a cuddle. Summer had guessed correctly—Bo was a cat person. Which was kind of interesting since Summer preferred felines, too.

Titan abruptly looked up. "Guys, I have some information on the diamonds. And it links straight back to that blond man who attacked your employee."

17

Bo SAT down on one side of Titan and I sat down on the other. "What is it?" I asked.

"We've confirmed that some rare diamonds went missing from an illegal mining operation in Sierra Leone last week. Reports confirm that a big blond man with a heavy European accent showed up in a village where they were doing mining for the militia. This man claimed he worked for the warlord and said he was sent to pick up their recent stash of diamonds. The villagers didn't believe him because they'd never seen him before." Titan took a deep breath. "He tortured some of the men until they agreed to open the safe in the on-site office. They said he took several handfuls of extremely valuable diamonds that could be easily concealed."

"A big blond man with an accent," I murmured. "He has to be the same guy who showed up in the cafe and at the hospital."

"Exactly. And he could very well be the man who broke into your employee's home. Thanks to Detective Hatcher's diligence in following up at the Greenbrier, we ran the man's name through INTERPOL and got multiple hits. Trust me, this ain't his first rodeo. Lucas Janssen is from Antwerp, Belgium, and he's connected with numerous international drug lords and jewel thieves."

"So he must've shipped the diamonds over to America, where they somehow made their way into a random security truck in West Virginia." Bo gave a whistle, which inspired Coal to respond with a short *woof*.

I stroked Coal's head, which was resting on my knee. "He wasn't talking to you, boy," I whispered.

"Not so random," Titan said. "He had to have accomplices. I'm sure Les was one of them—that's why he had to be killed. He knew there was more than bank money in that truck shipment. But Janssen would've had to have someone else on the inside—someone loading the truck."

"What about someone at the bank?" I asked.

"We're already looking into it," Titan said. "Detective Hatcher interviewed the two men involved with loading the money, but we might ask him to pull them back in for some more pointed questions."

"Good idea," Bo said, letting the wiggly kitty down to the floor. We all watched to see how Coal would react.

He didn't. He just kept his head on my knee as Stormy proceeded to tear off toward her cat tower and scratch the living daylights out of it.

"Good dog you have there," Titan said appreciatively.

I felt a burst of pride. "He sure is."

TITAN WARNED us to keep an eye out for Janssen at the cafe, although he assured us the FBI was actively trying to track the man down. When Titan stood and yawned, saying he needed to get back to his hotel, I noticed the circles under his eyes. Had he flown here? It hit me that I didn't even know where he was normally stationed.

When I stood to say goodbye, Coal sniffed at an invisible trail on the floor, casually inching closer to Stormy. He stopped about a foot away from the cat tower.

Realizing something was afoot, Stormy took a leap from her perch and landed square on Coal's nose.

Bo rushed for the kitten while I made a beeline to Coal. Stormy pranced around in a tidy circle on Coal's face as if she didn't have a care in the world. My poor dog stood, his strong jaw frozen shut.

Bo snatched Stormy up and scolded her, while I crouched next to Coal, patting his head and telling him what a good dog he was.

Titan, who'd watched the entire thing play out, clapped from the doorway. "You two have the most interesting pets I've ever met. Thanks for letting me drop in. I'll be in touch soon."

As he pulled the door shut behind him, I gave my brother a look. "You neglected to tell me that Titan was divorced."

Bo rubbed his thumb along Stormy's orange nose. "Was that important?"

So he *hadn't* been setting me up when he'd left Titan and me in the dust. His only intention was to get his running in for the night. I should've guessed as much. Bo was about as romantic as a pot of cold coffee.

"Nope. I just didn't know much about him, that's all." I slipped into my shoes. "Thanks for having me over. You driving us to church tomorrow?"

He nodded. "I'll pick you up. Then I want you to relax tomorrow afternoon, okay? I heard about how you passed out."

"*Nearly* passed out," I corrected him. "But yeah, that trailer wasn't a good scene to stumble onto. Plenty of blood, and you know how I am with blood."

"Gotcha," he said. "Hey, I have an idea. How about we head over to the tree farm? I know you haven't gotten a tree yet, and as you can see, neither have I. We need to get in the Christmas spirit, sis."

"You know what? You're right. I have that big bin of Auntie A's decorations up in the attic. Let's get that out...shoot, let's get a tree for Barks & Beans, too!"

"We could get some take-out and eat while we decorate," he added.

I couldn't help it. I threw my arms around his neck and squeezed him tight. I was going to say, "I love you," but I choked up.

"Love you too, sis," he whispered.

Sunday turned out to be one of those perfect days that made me wish I could relive it again and again. Church was relaxing and enlightening, then we headed home, changed, and hit the tree farm. After minimal arguing, we were able to agree on three trees. We set the smallest one up in the corner of the cafe's porch, in case any customers were allergic to pine.

While we listened to Christmas music and went through Auntie A's bin, Bo got a call from Titan. After talking a while, he hung up and reported what our agent friend had said.

It turned out Titan planned to stick around for one more day. He was going to sit in on the second interview with John Wright, the head banker. The FBI had discovered some discrepancies in the bank's records, and they seemed to point to Wright. I figured he had just earned himself a spot at the top of the suspect list.

In the meantime, flight records showed that Lucas Janssen had hopped a flight out of the country late Saturday night.

That would've been right after Les' murder. He'd managed to get a direct flight to Brussels. The FBI was working with Belgian authorities to track him down.

Once Bo shared what Titan had said, I gave a huge sigh of relief. "I didn't realize how stressed I was about that lunatic running around in our town until now," I said. "I mean, not only did he torture people in Sierra Leone, but then he came to the U.S. and wielded a grenade launcher, broke into the Goddards' house and choked Bristol, and finally shot and killed Les Stevens."

Bo hooked a nativity scene ornament toward the top of my tree. "It's a shame they didn't catch him before he got on that flight."

"He probably had help," I mused. "Titan said he had connections with all kinds of nefarious characters. And what about that dark-haired man who was asking questions—'Joe?' He must've stuck around."

Bo nodded. "I forgot to tell you that part. Titan said they're tracking him over here. The name he registered with at the Greenbrier was Walter Joseph, and they've located a con man who uses different variations of that name and operates on the East Coast. He's been involved in quite a few burglaries in the past, so I guess he's graduated to diamond theft. Facial recognition places him at a gas station heading northwest, toward Ohio. I figure he's long gone."

"Feliz Navidad" started playing on my music app, so I hit the thumbs-down to skip over it. I'd only heard it once today, and it was already stuck in my head. "So Bristol's out of danger now? And Clark and the rest of her family?"

"It would appear that way," Bo said. "I figure the police are trying to close the net on John Wright for his role in the attempted heist."

I placed my last star ornament on the tree, then sat on the

couch to admire the finished product. The tree didn't look professionally decorated by a long shot, but that made me love it even more. The homemade ornaments from our childhood brought back so many warm memories. As if sensing this was a special moment for me, Coal got up from his pillow and walked over to settle at my feet.

"Wait," I said, as realization dawned. "*Attempted* heist. Do you think Janssen ever found the diamonds that went missing? He went to a lot of trouble to retrieve them. And what about the money?"

"The fact that he left the country would indicate he got whatever he came for," Bo said. "Plus, Joseph is on the run, so he must've gotten paid."

"But that half a million...I wonder if Les and John Wright worked together and hid that somewhere? Then maybe Les refused to tell Janssen where it was when he got shot in the trailer."

Bo looked thoughtful. "That's a good question, but I'm sure Titan's checking into everything. I figure John Wright will be the missing piece in this puzzle, and like I said, they're about to lean on him *hard*."

I settled back against a pillow, enjoying the bright glow from the lights. "It takes a load off to know I don't have to watch Bristol like a hawk anymore," I said.

"No one told you to do that," Bo said. "We were only supposed to watch the cafe for Janssen." He closed the lid on the bin and sat down next to me. "You think I'm the protective one, but you have a mama bear streak a mile wide, Macy Jane Hatfield. I wouldn't want to mess with anyone you cared about." He gave Coal's head a pat. "Or any*thing* you cared about."

It snowed heavily in the night, blanketing my back yard. Knowing Bo would already be busy shoveling in front of the cafe, I hauled out my snow shovel and set to work on my back steps. Once those were scraped, I managed to clear a relatively decent path to the garden gate so Coal could do his business outside. This was definitely a day for my knee-high boots.

I let Coal out, then headed inside and threw on my work outfit, a couple strokes of mascara, and lipstick. I didn't have time for much more. After calling Coal in, I decided to use the connecting door to enter the cafe instead of tromping through the yard again. Summer was already standing in the Barks section, playing with the dogs. I walked in and froze in place when I recognized Waffles was part of today's canine crew.

"What—"

Summer turned. "Oh, no. This isn't what it looks like. I just didn't want to leave her out in the cold van. I'm taking Waffles to her foster family today. They seemed to hit it off with her, and now that they've gotten all the paperwork and doggie necessities in line, I'm dropping her off."

"That's good news." I managed to get moving again and walked over to pet Waffles' head. She nudged at my hand with her wet nose, but sat sedately in place. It would appear she was on her best behavior. Maybe she'd caught wind of a possible home in the works.

Summer stifled a yawn. "Sorry, I was up late with a foster kitten that couldn't settle in with my cats."

I noticed Summer hadn't even bothered to pull her hair into her regular ponytail. It really was a gorgeous honey color that set off her dark brown eyes. She was wearing jeans, which was also unusual, but she did have on a flowered blue shirt more in line with her boho style.

"Do you ever miss the purple hair?" I asked, recalling how

just a few months ago, Summer's hair had been a pale shade of violet.

"Nope. It was such a hassle to get it back to my regular color, and besides, I'm not into purple anymore."

Kylie piped up from the Beans section, where she was wiping down tables. "The purple worked for you, but I get it. Some things aren't easily erased." She turned back to her work.

Summer and I shared a look. Kylie's dragon tattoo basically owned the top half of her torso, meeting the back hairline underneath her dark bob and wrapping down both arms. Was she saying she regretted getting it? I knew there had to be a story behind her tattoos, and I hoped I could get close enough to the somewhat prickly barista to learn her motivations someday.

"Right." Summer pointed to the other three dogs. "The little one howls every now and then—she's part hound—but other than that, she just lies around. The medium sized brown one has some anxiety issues, probably from being abandoned out at Farmer Wheeler's place when it was snowy. And the big one..." She hesitated. "He has cataracts and he's way past his prime, unfortunately. If he doesn't get snagged soon, it's going to be the end of the road for him."

I knew Summer had been dreaming of transitioning her place into a no-kill shelter, but it meant she'd have to be more careful of which pets they accepted. And in our area, stray animals were still dropped off or reported to the shelter on a regular basis. Summer didn't have the heart to turn any of them away.

I tried to be cheery. "You've been doing a great job with the pet foster program, though. Surely between that and Barks & Beans, more pets are being adopted than ever."

"Oh, definitely," she said. "It's just when they get this old and sick, we know we can't afford to keep throwing our limited resources at them. I brought him here today just hoping someone would come in and bond. He's the sweetest dog." She leaned down and rubbed behind the dog's ears. I could tell he had been recently bathed, and his thick red-brown fur had been thoroughly brushed out. His near-blind eyes stared blankly into the distance, but he crept a little closer to my leg.

Summer brushed away a tear.

I think I did, too.

"I'm going to push him with the customers," I promised. "Does he have a name?"

"We've been calling him Edison. I have no idea why," she said.

"Got it. I think sharing the dogs' names kind of helps the customers see them as pets," I said.

"That makes sense." Summer untied her coat from her waist and shrugged into it. "Oh, and do you have what you need for Girl's Day Out? It's coming up soon."

After admitting I hadn't stocked the gift basket yet, we made a plan to meet up tomorrow night for final items. It would give us both something to look forward to.

When our first customer walked in, Waffles promptly launched into a barking frenzy. Bo, who was changing out of his snow-covered boots into work loafers, shot me a thinly-disguised glare.

Summer didn't miss it. She pulled Waffles' leash taut and beat a hasty retreat, edging around Bo on the way out the door.

How was I ever going to set those two up if my brother kept getting annoyed at Summer's shelter dogs? Then again, I supposed if it was meant to be, it would happen eventually. Auntie A always said you shouldn't rush love, and I always suspected she was referring to her teen marriage to Uncle Clive, a man who'd died in his fifties and left her with what seemed to be very few positive memories.

I was settling in with the remaining three dogs when someone familiar appeared in the cafe doorway.

Sheldia Powers looked a bit at sea as she stared at the menu choices. She'd been here at least once before, but she definitely wasn't a coffee aficionado. I heard her order a house coffee with cream and sugar just before Bo emerged from the back room.

Of course, her gaze traveled to my brother and locked in. Could she *be* any more obvious?

Bo tipped his head at her. "Sheldia, nice to see you."

She gave him a shy smile, then scooted down to the end of the bar to get out of the next customer's way.

Edison seemed to want to stick close. He stretched out by my feet, exposing his stomach so I could give it a rub. I peeked over the divider and watched as Sheldia awkwardly took a seat near the bookshelves. What a librarian move.

It hit me—this was the opportunity I hadn't even realized I had been waiting for. A chance to ask Sheldia a few more pointed questions about Black Friday.

Because as much as I wanted to believe her, I still got the feeling Sheldia hadn't been telling anyone the truth.

18

AFTER GIVING the dogs treats to keep them occupied for a few minutes, I left the petting area and made my way toward Sheldia's table.

Sheldia took a sip of her coffee and looked at me. "Hello, Macy."

I motioned toward the extra seat. "Do you mind if I sit down a sec?"

"Oh, of course. Please do." She set her cup on the table, revealing chipped fuchsia nail polish. Her black hair was in double braids, and she wore bibbed overalls and a plain T-shirt. Her smooth skin and oversized glasses added to the effect that she looked too young to drive.

It was unbelievable. She was in her forties, like Bo. I resolved to use a weekly face mask and up my water intake, in hopes of looking as good when I hit forty—which was just three years away.

I reeled in my thoughts. "Glad you got to stop by," I said. "Did you get to talk with my friend Summer about bringing shelter dogs to your Bookmobile visits?" I'd let her think this was the reason for my impromptu chat.

"I did, actually." She picked up the cup and adjusted the cardboard heat sleeve. "She was so nice. I think we'll work something out for January."

"Fantastic. Hey, how are those library backpacks coming along? I'd like to donate. And did you finish your foster care certification?"

Her face lit up, and it was transformative. She looked like a runway model. "We've already delivered some backpacks, but if you want to donate, that'd be fantastic because they're always needed. And yes! I did finish my foster classes and my home study was approved. I can't believe I'm saying this, but I'm ready for that first call."

I couldn't help but feel kindly toward her. Charity had told me a little about what was required to become a foster parent, and I knew it required some serious determination.

"That's wonderful." I had to force myself to broach the next topic. "I was thinking...you said an anonymous donor gave money for the new Bookmobile and backpacks?"

She nodded, sipping her coffee.

"So I guess they wanted to stay anonymous?" Had I really just followed up with such a dumb question?

She gave a slow nod. "Uh...yeah." She didn't elaborate.

One of the dogs gave a short bark, and I knew my interview time was over. I decided to make one last attempt to extract information from the tight-lipped librarian.

"I saw you on Black Friday...here, in the cafe," I said.

Her big blue eyes widened just a touch. "Oh, really? Yes, I think I did drop in that day. It was snowy, right?"

I nodded. "That was the day the security truck crashed, not far from here. Did you drive by it?"

Her ivory skin seemed to drain of color completely. "No, why?"

"I just wondered. They said a woman called for help from that pay phone on the street corner. I recalled you were in the cafe that day, and that your boots were muddy. I wondered if you'd gotten out of your car, maybe to check on the smoking truck, then you'd come into town to place that call."

She bristled. "Just because I had mud on my boots doesn't mean I was wandering around near the truck crash. As a matter of fact, I was walking my dog that morning, and it got away from me, so I slipped and fell in the slush. Those were my warmest boots, and I didn't have time to wipe them off before I headed out to shop."

A couple of yips sounded from the petting section, so I stood. "Oh, sure," I said. "It's been nice talking."

"Anytime," she said, but there was more than a hint of reserve in her tone.

It was only when I sat down next to Edison that I remembered Sheldia had recently declared that she wasn't ready to own a pet.

She didn't even *have* a dog.

THE DAY WAS WINDING DOWN, and I hadn't had any luck matching Edison with a new owner. The poor dog was lying on the mat, looking about as despondent as a dog could look, when an older woman strode into the petting area. She had that kind of British no-nonsense look about her, with her closely cropped white hair and sturdy walking shoes. As I stood to greet her, she held out a hand and gave mine a firm shake.

"I'm Cleo Burton. I've lost my husband recently," she

announced with no preamble. "I'm looking for a companion, a dog that isn't young and frisky. I had this feeling I should drop by your cafe today. I've only had those kinds of feelings a few times in my life, and I always live to regret it if I don't act on them. Am I right that you adopt dogs out? And do you have one that you think would fit the bill?" Her voice gave a little crack, and I saw straight through the bravado she was trying to project.

I smiled. "I think I might have the perfect dog for you. Edison, come here."

Not surprisingly, Cleo and Edison got on famously. I gave Cleo a bag of dog food on the house, then called Summer to let her know Cleo was coming. Bo helped load Edison into the older woman's car so she could drive directly to the shelter to adopt. Days like this reminded me of what the Barks & Beans Cafe was all about. Bo and I were bringing happiness into our corner of the world, one coffee drink and one perfect doggie match at a time.

Closing time finally rolled around, and our employees began to trickle home. I rarely worked days this long, from early morning until five, but since Bristol had been covering for me so much, I wanted to give her a break. Bo had already jogged home, but he'd left the keys to his extended cab truck with me so I could return the dogs to the shelter.

Once I'd closed out and cleaned up, I retrieved the dogs from the Barks section, where they'd been lounging. I headed toward the door, but someone knocked on it. Couldn't they see the *Closed* sign? I hesitated, glancing around for a weapon. All the sharp knives were locked in the back room. I peeked out the side window and breathed a sigh of relief.

Titan stood on the porch, twisting a wool cap in his hands.

When he caught sight of me—even though I'd thought I was fairly well-hidden—he gave a wave and pointed to the door.

"Okay, hang on," I shouted, unlocking the door.

Titan strode in, snow caked on the soles of his boots. As he moved closer to me, I had the feeling I needed to step back, not because he was going to harm me, but because he took up so much space.

"How tall are you?" I asked, then immediately wished I hadn't.

He chuckled. "Six five."

Good grief. And I thought Bo was tall at six foot one. Titan could fold up my five foot three self and tuck me into his pocket.

"Wow."

"Go ahead and say it," he said. Snow dusted his long, dark eyelashes.

Tugging on the dog leashes, I steered them back toward the petting area, so they could hang out while we talked. "Say what?" I had no idea what Titan meant.

"That my name fits. It was the first thing Bo said, after telling me he wasn't sure a Hatfield could get along with a McCoy like me."

"I've already done the Hatfield joke, and I've already asked if Titan was your real name," I said. "You told me your mom was into Greek myths, right?"

He loomed over me when I stepped out from the dog gate. "Exactly. But doesn't it seem weird that she gave me that name, and then—"

"You grew into this oversized giant," I finished.

He laughed outright. "You have a wicked sense of humor, Macy."

I grinned and gestured to a table. "Have a seat. Are you looking for Bo? He's already gone home."

He pulled out a chair, which looked almost doll-sized under his long frame. "Oh—I was hoping to go over some new developments with him on the heist case, maybe pick his brain a little."

"You're welcome to pick my brain," I said. "Bo will tell you I'm a good listener."

Titan grinned, but shook his head. "I'm sure you are, but since it's still an active investigation, I'm not really at liberty to discuss it with you right now."

I refused to be daunted. Of course, Bo always got special clearance because of his ex-DEA status, but I knew my brother wouldn't care if Titan filled me in. He knew how concerned I was about this case, given that Bristol and her family had been targeted. I sat up straighter. "Look, I'm sure Bo would want me to be aware of what was going on, especially if it involves Barks & Beans. I'm half-owner, you know?"

Titan nodded, his face impassive, although his eyes were warm. "Bo told me that. Sounds like a great fit for both of you."

I could tell he wasn't budging. "Hang on just a minute," I said, pulling my phone out of my pocket. "I'll call him."

Titan's eyes widened momentarily, but he settled back in his chair and watched me.

Bo picked up fairly quickly. "Hey, sis."

I briefly explained the situation. Bo chuckled at my determination, but said, "Hand the phone over to Big T, so I can talk to him." I did as he asked, trying not to look too smug as I placed the phone in Titan's hands. Bo and I were two Hatfields against one McCoy, after all.

It took a few minutes of heated discussion, but in the end, Bo won. Titan hung up and set my phone on the table. He eyed me shrewdly for a couple of seconds. "Well, your brother assures me you are the very soul of discretion."

I beamed.

Titan's lips twitched into a slow grin. "He also said you won't stop pestering him with questions about this case unless I keep you in the loop."

My wide smile died down a little. "He does have a point," I acknowledged.

Titan finally placed his hat on the table. With its somewhat imperfect stripes, it looked like someone had knitted it for him. I had to admit, it was kind of adorable that he went around wearing something so quirky.

He got serious. "We interviewed the banker today—John Wright."

"Yes?" I asked calmly, downplaying my eagerness to get the scoop. Had Wright made a deal with Les Stevens or Janssen?

He continued. "When Wright found out Stevens had been murdered, he panicked. He admitted he'd been involved in transferring the diamonds into the truck without listing them in the log book. When we asked why, he said that a while back, he and Stevens had gotten chatty at a bar, and when he was thoroughly drunk, Wright bragged about embezzling from his bank. He didn't even remember he'd done it until Stevens threatened blackmail if he didn't help him smuggle the diamonds onto his truck."

"That was pretty clever of Les," I said. "So Janssen shipped the diamonds into the country, they wound up at the bank, then Wright somehow made off with them before anyone saw them?"

"Exactly. Les' security company didn't run by the tightest standards, so it wasn't hard for Wright to slip the diamonds into the glove compartment. We're not talking about a big pile of diamonds that would be in a safe. So they could've easily been stolen, if someone knew where to look."

One of the dogs whined, ready to get back to the shelter. I stood. "So Janssen was going to stop the truck with the grenade launcher and retrieve the diamonds, but things went sideways when the truck slid off the road. Somehow, the diamonds must've gotten lost in the chaos of the wreck. Maybe Les swooped in and grabbed them then."

"That's what we're assuming." Titan grabbed his hat. He checked his phone before jumping to his feet. "I know you need to go. You want me to walk you home?"

"I actually have to return those guys to the shelter." I gestured to the dogs. "Don't worry, I'll fill Bo in on what you said."

"Wright filled in some blanks for us, that's for sure. He was supposed to get a cut on the sale of the diamonds, but he realized that Les and Janssen had just used him, with no intention to pay up." Titan tucked his chair in and waited while I leashed the dogs again. "Probably in that showdown in the trailer, Les admitted to Janssen where he'd hidden the diamonds. Then Janssen grabbed them and left the country."

"Maybe he got the money, too," I mused, leading the doggie crew toward the door. "So I guess that's a 'case closed' for you, huh? Are you heading back home? Come to think of it, where *is* your home?"

Titan held the door open for me. "I'm in a small town in central Virginia right now. It's a two and a half hour drive away. But I'll stick around one more day to wrap things up with Detective Hatcher."

I nodded, shivering in the cold outside air. I'd left my gloves at home, but maybe Bo had an extra pair in his truck. "Okay."

Titan followed me all the way out to Bo's truck, which was parked along the curb on the side street. Was there some reason he was sticking to me like white on rice? The villains had left the town—all except for the local banker, who'd seemed more than willing to cooperate with the police.

He helped me hoist the dogs into the cab section. I settled

into the driver's seat as the dogs began to lick snow from their paws. As usual, I had to slide the seat up to a position where I could actually reach the gas and brake pedals.

Titan's unusual eyes stayed focused on my face. "Uh...is there something you're not telling me?" I asked.

He frowned. "Wright told us he was sure that Janssen wasn't working independently. Someone sent him to Sierra Leone to get those diamonds, and someone helped him smuggle them to Wright. Wright never saw who brought the diamonds to the bank—he just retrieved them from a lockbox."

The dogs shifted behind me, bumping the seat. "Who owned the lockbox?" I asked. "Have you traced that?"

He nodded. "Actually, they just texted me. It was Christian Gill. The dead security truck driver."

19

"CHRISTIAN?" I repeated, dumbfounded. "He was working with Janssen? Then the wreck must've been unintended. But wouldn't he have known about the grenade launcher holdup and slowed down before he hit the icy patch?"

"These are the questions I'm asking myself," Titan said. He gave the truck door a solid pat. "You need to get going. Just know that for now, we have someone watching Clark's room. We're not sure if he was in on this or not, but given that he and Christian were allegedly close friends..." He shrugged.

I nodded. "I understand. And my lips will be sealed about Christian, especially with Della Goddard, because they'd dated a little."

"We were aware of that." He stepped onto the sidewalk and waved. "I'll see you soon."

As I pulled out, I mulled over what Titan had said. Someone had been calling the shots with that Sierra Leone robbery, but I found it hard to believe the mastermind was Christian Gill. Sure, he could've dropped the diamonds into his lockbox, but heading up an international hit? That seemed highly unlikely. It required a lot of money, and given the fact that Christian had been employed by—and didn't own—the security truck company, I couldn't see him sitting on a huge pile of wealth, even if his parents did own a restaurant chain, like Della had said. It didn't matter what I thought, though, because the FBI was probably scrutinizing Christian's financial records right now.

I had to consider Della again. How close had she and Christian been? Had she been lying to me, making up that whole story about the spilled contact solution causing her to pull off the road?

The idea that Della had taken me for a fool rankled me. I was still stewing over her possible lies when I pulled into the shelter.

Summer was working late, as usual. I knew it fell on her to clean up at the end of the day and walk the dogs. She welcomed me inside, but looked discouraged.

"Rough day?" I asked.

She nodded. "I guess I should've expected it, but Waffles is having some adjustment issues. The family is going to give her another day, but if she keeps up this behavior, I'm afraid that next thing you know, she'll be back here."

I helped her return the other two dogs to their kennels, trying not to picture Waffles' sad eyes. "What kind of adjustment issues?"

"Just like she did in my house, she went to the bathroom on their rugs a couple of times, even though she's house trained and she's never had accidents at the shelter."

"Maybe she's nervous to be in a new place," I said.

The cacophony of dog barks was starting to drown out our voices, so Summer gestured to the main room. I followed her out.

"I think you're right," she said, stepping behind the desk to shut down her computer. It was a huge old desktop model, probably running on an outdated system. I wished I had lots of extra money to donate to the shelter so they could update the place. Maybe someday.

"Don't give up," I said. "Sometimes it just takes time. When I was a kid, I had this mutt named Jesse James. Yes, that was his name, because he acted like an outlaw. When he was a puppy, he wouldn't do his business outside. It was like he held it until he got back in the house. But at some point, things clicked for him, and he turned out to be one of the best dogs we ever had."

"I hope that's the case." Summer flicked her bangs from her eyes. "Hey, great job placing Edison, by the way. I was so excited to meet Cleo and see how they'd already connected. I thought his earthly days were about over, but I figure this friendship will help them both."

"Oh, I agree. So this day was a victory, at least in one aspect."

Summer nodded. "I can't wait to shop with you tomorrow night. You want to grab food first?"

"Definitely." It would give me more time to catch up with my busy friend. "I'll call you then."

I headed out so Summer could finish locking up. Once I'd jumped in the truck and turned on the heat, my phone rang.

It was Della.

I tried to keep my voice level as I answered. "Hey."

She sounded tired. "Hey there. Listen, I keep thinking about what happened in the trailer. I just need someone to talk to, and you were the only one who saw everything. Do you mind stopping over sometime? Actually—I'm at home tonight, and I made a huge chicken casserole and salad. You're welcome to join us."

It couldn't be some kind of trap if her kids were around, I supposed. Maybe she was feeling guilty and wanted to unload on someone, especially if she had been in on the heist with Christian and knew she was at least indirectly responsible for the deaths of Christian and Les, not to mention her brother's coma.

"Sure, I'll drop by. I need to head home and walk Coal first, then I'll be over—give me about twenty minutes?"

"Sounds good," she said.

Bo wasn't in when I dropped off his truck, so I figured he was out for a run. I texted to let him know where I was heading, in case he noticed my car was gone—which he usually did.

After getting Coal squared away, I headed over to Della's place, unsure how to get more information on Christian from her. Maybe I could get her talking about dating. When I rang the doorbell, Bristol met me.

"Hey there! I made this absolutely *gigantor* salad, and Mom made my favorite casserole, so I'm so glad you came to help us eat tonight!" Her dark, glossy hair tumbled around her shoulders.

"Me, too," I said, always happy to see my bubbly employee.

Della welcomed me into the kitchen, and I had a seat at the table. There were only three plates set. "Where's Ethan?" I asked.

"He's been pretty tired and out of sorts lately, so he's eating in his room tonight." Della put on two big oven mitts and carried the casserole over, setting it squarely on a crocheted potholder. "I can tell he's ready for his dialysis, but it's not until tomorrow."

"I'm sorry to hear that," I said, holding up my glass so Bristol could pour ice water into it.

"I never thought I'd say this, but I'm thankful for the internet. He finds all these brain games online, and they keep him occupied."

Bristol nodded, taking a seat next to me. "Only he's already too smart for his own good. Did you know he got a perfect score on the Math section of his ACT?"

"That's amazing," I said. "Does he have plans for college?" It was only *after* I'd asked that I realized Ethan probably wasn't in good enough health to attend college, and on top of that, Della probably couldn't afford to pay for it, anyway.

Della placed an enormous scoop of casserole on my plate, giving me a brave smile instead of a direct answer. "He's always been so clever. Did you know he was homeschooled all the way through? Only I can't take all the credit—around ninth grade he basically started teaching himself, and he's already taken a lot of online college classes." Her quiet voice gained strength. "He should be able to get scholarships so he can do full-time college online. And once Clark's able to go back to work..." She fell silent as she scooped salad into bowls, as if she'd run out of steam.

"How is Clark?" I asked, hoping he hadn't had any setbacks. "Has he been talking much?"

Bristol nodded, her dark eyes bright. "He talks a little more each day. Not about the wreck, though."

Della finished pouring dressing on her salad. "Let's pray," she said. She bowed her head and gave a quick word of thanks. Once she finished, I waited for her to take the first bite before I dug in.

"It's delicious," I said, meaning it. Della was a knockout cook.

We made casual conversation until Bristol polished off her meal, then she begged off to watch *Lost*, which she said she'd been bingeing for a solid month.

I grinned. "You just opened up a whole new world of conversation with me, girlie. Don't even get me started on John Locke."

"No spoilers!" Bristol broke into a silly sprint up the hallway.

Once Bristol was out of sight, Della heaved a sigh and met my eyes. "I'll admit I'm having a hard time with this. First Christian died, then Clark was in the coma, and now Les dies right in front of me. I keep wondering who's next."

I wanted to reassure her that Janssen had left the country and Joseph had fled, so neither would pose a further threat to her family, but Titan hadn't given me clearance to do that. Besides, maybe this was all some sob story act and she was perfectly aware of where her criminal cohorts had run off to.

I set my glass down. "I can tell you miss Christian. What was he like?"

She smiled. "He was this big, likeable guy. Kind of goofy, you know? He still lived with his parents, but he had his own little place behind their pool. He wasn't super ambitious, just wanted to do what made him happy, and for some reason, driving a security truck did."

He didn't sound like the kind of guy who'd try to set up a bank truck heist, but maybe Della was downplaying his brilliance. "I'll bet his parents are devastated," I said.

She blinked back tears. "They are. I think they're going to set up some kind of scholarship in his name."

All the sweet thoughts in the world didn't change the fact that Christian had placed those smuggled diamonds in his lockbox at the bank. I tried to resolve the two versions of Christian in my mind, but couldn't find any success.

Della dabbed at her eyes with a napkin. "I don't know about you, but I keep replaying that day in the trailer in my head. Why did Les want *me* there? Why not call one of his friends?"

"I have a feeling Les didn't have many friends." I thought back to what Les had told Della when he called. "Didn't he say he wanted to tell you something that might interest your brother Clark?"

She nodded.

I hesitated, trying to think through how to word things. "What if—and I know it sounds crazy—but what if Clark could've been involved in the heist?"

She stared at me like I was out of my mind. "Clark? Never!"

Ethan stalked into the kitchen. His earbuds were in, and he merely gave me a passing wave before piling more casserole on his plate.

Della barely waited until he got back to the hallway. She shoved her chair back and stood. "I think maybe you'd better go now. You seem to be accusing my brother of being a criminal."

I stayed seated, hoping she'd calm down. "That's not what I'm saying. But why would Les have mentioned Clark specifically, do you think?"

"I assumed it had to do with his job—probably his insurance." She let out a breath and returned to her seat. "Listen, I know you mean well, and you've looked out for Bristol so much. Trust me, I have lots of questions for Clark when he starts talking more. But I promise, I've told you the extent of what I know. I'm not hiding anything." Her dark eyes flashed with intensity. "I'm not going to push my brother to talk before he's ready. I'm honestly not even sure how much he remembers about the wreck."

I had to admit defeat. Della was a concerned sister, and she was protective of her brother, that was all. Wouldn't I act the same way in her shoes? Maybe Christian had been involved in the heist, but I couldn't believe Della would ever risk her brother's life for money—or diamonds.

"Thanks for the delicious meal." I pushed my chair back. "Now, how about I help you clean up, then we'll talk some more."

Della gave me a warm smile, and it felt like the sun was shining on me. She placed a hand on mine. "Thanks for understanding."

Whether it was a strength or a weakness, I still couldn't say, but being understanding was one of my strongest traits. Jake had used my empathetic nature against me more than once. But I didn't get the feeling Della was using me. In fact, I got the feeling she wanted to be friends.

I'd been so alienated in my marriage with Jake. But since I'd moved home, new friends seemed to be walking into my life left and right.

I couldn't see any good reason to shut them out.

20

I STAYED LATE at Della's, learning more about her life. She seemed to want to unburden herself, and not just about Les' death. She talked about her husband's fatal heart attack and how she spun out afterward. Clark had stepped up to be there for her children, more than once.

I broached the subject of dating after marriage, and we had more than one laugh about our attempts to catch up with the latest social media trends. Neither of us were online savvy.

"I went on this one date where I took a bathroom break and texted Bristol about how boring the guy was. Only guess who got the text?" Della grinned. "You guessed it. My date. Suffice it to say, we didn't go out again."

Ethan jaunted into the kitchen again, grabbing a bag of chips. "You know I'm happy to help you with technology, Mom."

"Thanks, but you know it's pretty hopeless," she said.

My phone buzzed with a text. Bo asked if I was back yet and said the roads were getting icy. I shot a reply that I was heading out now before slipping my phone into my purse.

"I'd better get going," I said. "Thanks for talking, Della. Let's do this again soon."

After saying our goodbyes, I crunched out to my car on the iced over sidewalk. It was a good thing Bo had put my snow tires on just before Thanksgiving. I let my engine idle a little, then tried to turn on the heat. As I expected, it blasted cold air. I switched it to defrost and pulled out.

This late at night, usually no one was on the roads. But someone pulled out from a space behind me and seemed to be gaining ground quickly.

"Why're you in such a hurry?" I said aloud. The driver continued to ride my bumper, as if looking for an opportunity to pass on the one-lane road.

Unwilling to push my speed due to the black ice on the road, I finally gave up and pulled over alongside a sidewalk.

To my horror, the driver pulled off just behind me. So much for convincing myself this wasn't personal.

I didn't hesitate, turning the wheel and pulling back into the middle of the road. My car skidded a little, but soon gained traction, so I gave it more gas.

Unfortunately, the other car followed me. My mind raced. I knew better than to lead the person to my house. But where could I go this time of night? Was the police station even open?

I made a snap decision. There *was* one place I could go, anytime of the day or night.

I drove straight to Bo's house and swung into the parking space just behind his truck. Without checking to see if the vehicle was still following me, I laid on the horn.

It took approximately three seconds for Bo to flip on his front porch light and emerge. He peered out until he saw my car, then he held to the railing, walking down the icy steps toward me. I was sure he was fully armed under his coat.

Only when he got to my side window did I dare to turn.

No cars were parked behind me—not one. Had I missed seeing the stalker pass me? Or had he turned off a side road at the last minute?

My arms started shaking as I explained what had happened to Bo. I knew I wasn't very helpful, since I had no idea what kind of vehicle had been tailing me.

"Maybe they were trying to scare you," he said.

"Well, it worked." I rubbed at my arms.

He climbed into the passenger seat. "Just drive me back to your place. I'll walk you in."

"But what about your house? They'll probably assume I live there, and maybe they'll come back."

Bo gave a laugh that wasn't at all friendly. "I *dare* them to step foot in my house."

I let out a breath and edged the car back into the street. It was true, Bo could take care of himself. But could I?

When we got home, Coal definitely sensed my unease. I let him out for a bathroom break and he seemed to do his business in record time. He skidded back up on the porch and scratched at the door. I opened it, and he bolted straight upstairs to his bed.

In the meantime, Bo had retrieved my .22 from my gun safe. He had me practice with the safety and action a couple of times before loading it and placing it in easy reach near my bed. He assured me that although he planned to check the cars along our street on his way home, he figured no one had followed us here.

"I'll let Detective Hatcher know tomorrow," he said. "I figure it was some joker looking for a woman out this time of night. He realized you weren't an easy catch. It's disturbing, but not completely unheard of. You're out of harm's way now, but would you feel better staying at my place?"

"No." I tried to project more confidence than I felt. "I'll be fine here—I have Coal and the .22."

He pulled me into a quick hug, his eyes tired. "Okay. Lock up well after me. Keep my number pulled up on your phone, just in case. But Coal will let you know if anyone tries to break in, won't you, boy?" He petted behind Coal's ears.

Coal was sitting on the alert, obviously not planning on going to sleep anytime soon. I couldn't deny that he was able to pick up on my moods.

"Thanks, Bo," I said, following him downstairs. "You stay safe, too."

As I locked up, I tried to shake off my continued jitters. Bo was most likely right; it was probably some late night ne'er do well. They could've even been on drugs.

But why did it feel so ominous, so targeted, like someone knew I was at the Goddards' house?

SOMEONE WAS KNOCKING at my door. Not using the doorbell, just knocking. Coal had already positioned himself squarely in the center of my bedroom doorframe. He looked back at me and gave a quiet bark, just to keep me abreast of the situation, I supposed.

I rubbed at my eyes. The sun wasn't even out. My phone clock read six twenty. I wasn't on duty today at the cafe, so Bo would know better than to wake me up in person at this hour.

Still, if someone wanted to break in, why would they knock first? I reluctantly put on my frog slippers and grabbed the .22, just in case. After flipping on the hall light, I followed Coal downstairs.

I hit the kitchen light and looked out my small back window. A tall man in a knit cap stood on the porch.

Titan.

I unlocked the doors and ushered him in, regretting that he had to catch sight of my beat-up footwear. He didn't seem to notice. Concern etched his features.

"Bo texted me about what happened to you last night. He's told Detective Hatcher, too. I just wanted to hear what happened from the horse's mouth, so to speak."

"Sure." I backed up, allowing room for him to take his boots off. "I take it you haven't eaten breakfast yet?"

He shook his head. "The continental breakfast at the hotel often leaves something to be desired. Fake sausage patties and powdered eggs don't really appeal, you know?"

I pulled out my French press. "I hear ya. I'm going to make us some coffee, and I can throw some eggs on to boil, if that works?"

"Perfect," he said.

As I prepped the makeshift breakfast, Coal climbed onto his pillow in the living room, pawed it into the shape he wanted, then plopped onto it and promptly went back to sleep.

"He definitely likes you," I said. "He's not even paying attention to you, which shows his acceptance. Did you have dogs growing up?"

"Not really. But I did run with a rough crowd, so let's just say I'm not easily scared. Maybe he picks up on that." He took a sip of coffee and smacked his lips. "This is great. Why doesn't mine ever taste this way?"

"It's the power of the French press," I said. "It's practically foolproof if you put the right amount of quality coffee in."

I went on to tell him, blow by blow, about what the stalker had done last night. When I finished, Titan looked perplexed. "Detective Hatcher said they haven't had any issues with attacks on women or robberies at night lately. It seems a little too coincidental."

"You think they targeted me because I was at the Goddards'?"

"Maybe." He cut his egg in half and sprinkled salt on it, then pepper.

"Things seem to keep pointing back to them," I said. "But I talked with Della last night—don't worry, I didn't mention anything about Christian's involvement with the heist. I really believe her when she says she's not involved, and she doesn't think Clark was, either."

"She's his sister. Of course she's going to say that." He took a huge bite of egg, leaving only a tiny piece behind.

"Maybe. But she really does seem oblivious."

"The fact remains that Janssen and his cohort Walter Joseph broke into the Goddards' early in the game. For some reason, they believed something was hidden there. Now, maybe Les had given them the wrong idea, not dreaming they'd resort to a break-in."

I huffed. "Knowing the kind of guy Les was, I'll bet he didn't care that he'd put the Goddard family in danger. He just wanted his disreputable friends to leave him alone so he could hide the diamonds."

Titan nodded and drained his cup. "Still, it doesn't make sense anyone would be camped outside their house now, since Janssen must've recovered the diamonds before he fled to Brussels."

"Maybe my stalker doesn't know anything about Janssen—maybe he just read about the money going missing, and he's trying to track *that* down. And speaking of Brussels, have the Belgian police caught Janssen yet?"

"I hope to hear something today." He stood, and Coal ambled over to his side, hoping for a pet. "I'll head out now.

Sorry for bombing in here so early, but I just wanted to follow up with you."

"Thanks," I said. "I appreciate it."

As I closed the door behind him, I felt more apprehensive than I had last night. The fact that Titan had gotten involved meant that everything hadn't settled down like I'd hoped. There were loose ends, and people were running around town trying to scare me or worse.

But who?

21

I shoved all the dishes in the dishwasher and trudged upstairs for a shower. Just as I'd grabbed some clothes, my phone rang. There was no name, just a number from Louisiana. Probably a telemarketer. I let it go and climbed into the shower.

Once I'd toweled off, I glanced at the phone, surprised to see the spammer had left a message. Vaguely curious, I hit the speaker button and pushed play before shoving my arms into my shirt.

A woman's voice filled the line. She had a heavy southern drawl. "Well, hello there, Macy. I tried to get a message to you last night, but you didn't stop long enough for my man to give it to you." She giggled. "Guess he scared the bejeebers out of you, didn't he? I'd say I'm sorry, but I'm not." Her voice hardened. "If you want to avoid another run-in with my friend, you're going to get some information for me."

What on earth was this? I continued to play the message, unsure where she could possibly be going.

"Now, you seem to be friendly with the Goddards. Close, even. I heard that Clark woke up from his unfortunate coma.

What you're going to do is pay him a little visit. I need you to find out where he hid my goods."

Was she talking about the diamonds? She must not know Janssen already took them. Who was this woman?

Her drawl continued. "Once you get that information, you're going to call me at this number. You're not going to tell your brother or anyone else a thing. Yeah, I know all about your brother, honey." She gave a short laugh. "He's a regular burr in my husband's side. But let's not talk about that. You call me back by tomorrow, okay? Bye."

I replayed the message a couple of times, in complete shock. The woman had called Bo a burr in her husband's side, and there was only one criminal I knew was my brother's sworn enemy.

Leo Moreau.

She had to be his *wife*.

AFTER DOWNING another cup of coffee, I came to a decision. It wouldn't hurt to ask Clark some questions, would it? If I discovered anything, I'd tell Titan first. If I didn't, I'd call the number and tell the woman she was barking up the wrong tree. She must not know about Janssen, so I could always point her in the general direction of Brussels.

Sure. I'd just call and chat up the wife of an arms dealer. No biggie.

I gave Coal some food and told him goodbye. Grabbing my keys and purse, I headed out to the car. Most of the cars parked along the sidewalk belonged to neighbors, and it didn't look like anyone was lurking in a vehicle, but I still had the feeling I was being watched.

Why didn't this woman just send her own henchman over

to the hospital? Maybe she guessed someone was standing guard there?

Della called just as I slid into my seat. "Hey, Macy. You were so faithful to care for us when Clark was in a coma, I wanted you to be one of the first to know they're releasing him today. I'm heading over to pick him up now."

Now what? I needed a pretense to talk with him.

"That's wonderful! Thanks for letting me know. I could grab some lunch for you from the cafe and drop it off," I offered.

"No need," Della said. "I have leftover casserole, and that's one of Clark's favorites. We'll grab some lunch at home, then I'm going to run over and pick Ethan up from dialysis."

"Okay." I took another wild stab. "Does Clark need someone to sit with him while you pick up Ethan? I know Bristol's at work."

"That's so sweet of you, but Clark's already said he's ready to kick back and play his favorite video game. He just wants to relax without all the machines beeping and the hospital commotion."

So much for that. "Of course," I said. "I'm happy for you all."

"I appreciate everything you've done. Gotta run."

After hanging up, I reluctantly got out of my car and headed back into the garden. I didn't seem to have any choice but to call Moreau's wife and tell her I couldn't get close to Clark.

As I put the key in the lock, I paused. Coal gave an anxious yip, making it obvious he was waiting just behind my door.

I *did* have a choice. I could tell Titan everything. That way, I wouldn't be putting Bo in danger. Titan would know what to do.

I sat down on the porch chair and scrolled down for Titan's number, but my phone rang.

Ethan's name popped up on the screen. Maybe he wanted to let me know about Clark.

"Hey there," I said. "I heard about your uncle."

He spoke quietly. "I know, it's great, isn't it? But I was actually calling because I needed you to do something for me, if you don't mind."

He probably needed something brought over to him, since his mom was headed for the hospital and his sister was at work. "Sure. I'm happy to help."

"It's kind of a long story," he said. "You know I'm at home most of the time, and I'm pretty easily bored. I like challenges, you know?"

Maybe he needed me to bring over some of those brain games his mom talked about. "Right," I said, hoping to hurry him up. I needed to call Titan.

His voice lowered. "See, the thing is, I took a few online courses and I kind of learned how to hack."

"Hack?" I repeated.

"Like, computer hacking, you know? So I thought it'd be fun to hack into Les Stevens' office computer. It was easy enough when Uncle Clark took me to his office Halloween party. Thing is, I found some weird stuff on there."

Ooh, probably Les had been a pervert, as well. "That's too bad."

"He was on the dark web—you know, a place where criminals hang out."

"Wait—you've been on the dark web?" A teenager, trolling around with villains?

His voice dropped to a whisper. "Trust me, I didn't stay on there long. But I found this string of emails between Les and some dude named Lucas Janssen. It seems like Les was looking to make money fast because Stevens Security was on shaky financial ground. Lucas said he'd be willing to work with him to get some diamonds into the country. All Les had to do was to find someone in the bank to shift Janssen's diamonds into a hidden place in one of his security trucks. Janssen said he'd do the rest."

Oh, no. Ethan knew entirely too much. "Why are you telling me all this?" I asked.

"Hang on, let me finish," he said. "The banker's job would be to stash the diamonds in the front of the truck while Clark and Christian loaded the back. Janssen said the diamonds would be in five sealed honey mustard containers, and they'd need to be placed in the glove compartment."

Holy moly. This kid...

"Why haven't you told the cops?" I demanded.

"I'm getting to it," he said. "Listen—" His voice dropped off and I could hear someone else talking in his room. He returned to the line. "I've gotta go because the nurse is here." He gave a cough and spat out the words "dog fence." Then my line went dead.

I sat there, stunned. Ethan had known all along about the diamonds, but he'd never said a word. Maybe he'd hoped to get them for himself? And why did he say *dog fence* when he didn't even have a dog?

I opened the door and let Coal out to use the bathroom. It was still cold, but not enough to force me inside. Coal slid on a tiny section of ice that lingered on the pathway, then took off toward the back of the garden.

I was about to call Titan when I had a thought. Surely Ethan hadn't meant the dog fence outside Barks & Beans? Had he also intercepted one of Les' messages that disclosed where he'd hid the diamonds?

It was worth checking, I decided, even though I knew Janssen had already retrieved the gems. Verifying that they weren't hidden in the fence would allow me to confidently point Moreau's wife toward Janssen. Of course, I'd tell Titan first so he could bug the phone before I called her.

I let Coal back in the house, then headed for the cafe. I knew Bo was going to have questions, and sure enough, he met me as I walked in.

"What's going on?" he asked, stealing a quick look at Bristol, who was busy with the dogs. "Everything okay?"

"It's fine," I said. "I just had to check on something out in the dog run."

He nodded and headed back to the coffee bar. Jimmy was working, and he gave me a quick smile before turning to the espresso machine.

I hurried into the Barks section and said a brief hello to Bristol. "I hear your uncle's getting out today," I said. "That's great news."

She smiled. "I know! I'm planning to make stuffed shells tonight for him."

"Good for you," I said. "I just need to head outside real quick."

She gave me a quizzical look, but didn't ask questions. "Sure."

Once I'd firmly closed the side door, I looked at the fenceline. It attached to the cafe and ran down to where it met the neighbor's stone wall. Stepping closer, I paced along the white slats, looking for holes in the ground or packages tucked in near the posts, but there was nothing. Finally, I reached the end, where the fence was bracketed onto the stones. Blackberry brambles had sprung up and hidden the stone wall. We needed to get in there and hack those out.

I pulled out my cell phone flashlight and tried to peer into the underbrush, but it was too dense. The only place I could imagine someone hiding something would be in the rock crevices near the fence, so I put my gloves on before plunging my hand in, hoping I didn't run into a brown recluse. At least snakes wouldn't be out this time of year.

I was about to call it quits when my gloved finger tapped something. I shoved my left hand into the space, using both hands to retrieve the object and slide it out.

The moment it came into the light, I gasped.

It was a honey mustard packet, sealed tight.

Had I actually stumbled onto the diamonds? It couldn't be that simple. I took off my glove and peeled back the foil, my hands trembling.

Inside the packet, which had been filled with a gel that *looked*, but didn't smell like honey mustard, someone had indeed tucked a handful of glittering, cut gemstones. The yellow gel effectively insulated the diamonds from rattling against each other. I carefully extracted a couple, wiping them off before placing them in my palm. The sunlight hit them, sending brilliant beams everywhere. I stared at the valuable jewels, transfixed. They had been cut large, maybe four to five carats in size. Just this one packet must be worth...I had no idea. Especially if they were top quality color and had minimal flaws.

I'd learned quite a bit about diamonds when Jake and I had shopped for my engagement ring. It had been a showstopper—a two carat emerald cut that was impossible to miss. Flashy like Jake, I supposed. But the funny thing was that when Jake told me he was leaving, I didn't feel one twinge of regret as I stuffed the ring in a box and told him to keep it.

Huge diamond rings were actually cheap when compared to the cost of loving someone so deeply you kept your vows. That was a price Jake wasn't willing to pay.

"Sis?" Bo's voice interrupted my thoughts.

I nearly dropped the diamonds. "What? Oh, yeah—"

He stepped toward me before I could hide what I was holding. "What's that?"

"We need to talk," I said.

Bo DIDN'T WASTE any time in calling Titan and getting him on the scene. Together, we hunted through the brush and uncovered four more packages of diamonds, just like Ethan had said.

"Why do you think Ethan called you?" Titan asked.

"All he said was that he wanted me to do something for him. Then, when he told me what he'd uncovered on the dark web, I figured he was going to ask me to tell the cops about it so he wouldn't get in trouble for hacking. But then he mentioned the diamonds...and he told me where to find them."

Titan sat on a bench we'd recently picked up at a yard sale. He'd worn jeans and a hoodie, which made him look more approachable. "He's going to contact you again, if he knew the diamonds were there."

Bo nodded. "Maybe he *put* them there, sis."

I shook my head. "I find that hard to believe."

Titan looked grim. "The fact remains that Ethan isn't trustworthy."

I took a deep breath. "I have some more news. I got a phone message and an ultimatum from a woman I'm fairly certain is Leo Moreau's wife."

Bo's eyebrows lowered and his jaw tightened.

"Anne Louise Moreau," Titan murmured. "She's a piece of work."

"How so?" I asked.

"Let's just say she has her own henchmen, and they're probably more loyal than Leo's men," he said.

"I gathered that," I said. "She basically said one of her men followed me in the car last night. And she told me to get information out of Clark Graham or she'd sic her guy on me again."

"That's not going to happen." Bo shot a wild look around, like he needed something to pummel.

"What were your specific instructions?" Titan asked.

I played the message, so they could hear how Anne had asked me to call her back without telling Bo what was going on.

"She wishes," Bo said. "You involve my sister, you involve me, punk."

Titan held up a large hand. "Hang on. We can use this to trap her, Bo. We'll feed her false information."

It sounded like a solid plan, but I had a feeling there was more than one way it could go wrong.

22

TITAN FINAGLED a way to remotely tap my phone, then gave me detailed instructions of what to say when I called Ethan back. The FBI needed to know if Ethan had personally played a role in the diamond heist. I couldn't see how a mostly housebound teen with polycystic kidney disease could've outwitted an international diamond smuggler, but I'd already underestimated Ethan once. The kid was obviously brilliant, playing brain games and hacking into the dark web.

"Once we find out how deeply Ethan is involved, if at all, we'll lay the trap for Anne Moreau," Titan said. "We'll tell her where the diamonds are hidden—of course they won't be there —and figure out a way to make it seem like she's the only one who can retrieve them. Then we'll have her."

Something told me things wouldn't be as easy peasy as Titan made them sound, but I was ready to do what needed to be done. Bo had to go back into the cafe to work, so in order not to create a scene in front of Bristol, Titan and I slipped out the front gate onto the sidewalk. We took a quick jog around the cafe to my back garden.

I let both of us into the house, where Coal greeted us with enthusiastic tail wagging. I petted Coal's head and Titan hesitantly followed suit. Coal gave a grunt of pleasure like he wanted to say a word of thanks.

"Time to get to work," I said, shooing Coal toward his pillow. I gestured toward the couch and Titan took a seat.

After settling in the chair directly across from him, I pulled out my phone and called Ethan.

"Hi, there," I said. "We didn't get to finish our conversation."

"Sorry I didn't have time to explain," he said. "I had to stay longer than I thought today, but Bristol's coming to pick me up this evening. What I was saying is that I need you to check into the corner of that dog fence at your cafe. At Barks & Beans."

I tried to sound innocent. "Why?"

He whispered, "Because that's where I hid the diamonds."

My heart sank. So he *had* somehow intercepted the smuggled diamonds. "But when were you ever at the cafe?" Hopefully, he hadn't dragged Bristol into this mess, too.

"You should know—I bumped into you the day I hid them," he said. "Just outside the cafe."

In a flash, I recalled the teen in the scarf and hooded coat who'd brushed past me on Black Friday. *That* had been Ethan?

He continued to explain. "See, I walked into town that day and met up with Uncle Clark outside the bank. I asked if I could hang out with him a little. He didn't guess that our meeting wasn't happenstance. While he and Christian were loading the back, he asked me to stay out of their way. That worked out perfectly, because I was able to stand just out of sight and watch for Mr. Wright to hide the diamonds." He chuckled. "I wasn't sure how he was going to get in since the cab was locked, but he told Christian some story about a paper he'd forgotten to get. Christian unlocked the door for him, then went back to work loading. I guess he trusted Mr. Wright since he was a banker. Once Mr. Wright finished stashing the diamond packets in the glove compartment, he closed the door and headed back into the bank. I took my opportunity and ran over and grabbed the diamonds."

"Wow." It was the only thing I could think to say. It was unbelievable that Ethan had been so premeditated about the heist, although I wondered what his alternate plan would've looked like if Christian had locked the cab door again.

"It *is* pretty crazy." It was clear he was proud of his craftiness. "Anyway...after I pocketed the diamonds, I told Uncle Clark I was getting tired and I was going to walk home. On the way, I noticed the fence at your cafe and realized it was as good a place as any to hide the diamonds until I could pick them up. I knew I shouldn't keep them on me, just in case the theft was discovered quickly."

"So Christian and Clark had no idea what was going on?" I asked.

"None," Ethan confirmed. Genuine regret filled his tone. "I'm not sure why their truck went off the road, but it might've had something to do with the diamonds."

I didn't want to make Ethan feel worse by confirming that was the case. "But what were you going to do with the diamonds, once you picked them up?"

His tone brightened a little. "I'm still getting them, remember? I just need you to pick them up for me, since I can't get out of here until later and this is probably an opportune time. I'll let you keep a couple of diamonds for your trouble, if you promise not to tell anyone. I know you've really been there for my mom, so I figured you were trustworthy."

He was one to talk about being trustworthy, having kept his mouth shut the entire time about his involvement in the truck heist. An involvement that had jeopardized the safety of everyone he loved, from his uncle to his sister.

"What do you need diamonds for, Ethan? Why not tell the police about them?" I asked.

"I already have things lined up. I'm going to help my family. I can't talk right now, but please find those honey mustard packages for me. I've been following the news, and the police just said Janssen stole the diamonds and made off with them, so they're not going to be looking at me. I need to get them back so I can sell them to a buyer I know is interested."

I wanted to tell Ethan that he'd been playing with fire and he was definitely going to get burned, but Titan put a finger to his lips, urging me to play along. "Uh, okay. I'll get them. Where and when should we meet up?"

"I don't drive yet, and we can't meet at my house since Uncle Clark will be back and things will be hectic. Bristol can drive me to meet you somewhere. Someplace private. How about your place? Don't you live behind the cafe?"

"I do, but I'm not so comfortable bringing those diamonds into my house, Ethan." I nodded at Titan. We'd talked things through beforehand, in case Ethan did admit to hiding the diamonds and wanted to meet for a drop. "Let me think...there's this cemetery as you get toward the interstate—you know the one? We could meet there, and chances are no one would be around."

"Sure, I know it. It's not far from here. We'll probably get out of here around six. Will the cemetery be open then?"

"I'm pretty sure it stays open until seven, so it should work fine. It's really well-lit, too. I'll meet you by that big mausoleum area in the middle—*if* I find the diamonds. If not, I'll call you."

Ethan gave a short laugh. "There's no 'if.' I hid those diamonds myself. I know they'll be there. I'll see you then."

As I hung up, I couldn't disguise the sadness that crept into my voice. "He did it," I said. "He swiped the diamonds after Wright put them in the truck."

Titan shook his head. "Poor kid—he's gotten in over his head. Though it does speak well for him that he chose *you* to retrieve the diamonds and bring them to him. He's certainly very trusting."

"Too trusting by a long shot," I said. "His mom would be appalled. I'm sure Ethan hasn't even grasped all the ways he's exposed himself and his entire family to serious danger."

"Exactly," Titan said. "He's been messing with the big leagues of crime. There's no way he can protect himself. Now, we need to go over the plan for the cemetery, because you know I'll be coming along for the ride."

AFTER BRIEFING me on the plan, Titan called Bo on speakerphone and filled him in on recent developments. Of course, Bo wanted to come along, but Titan asked him to stay at the cafe and close up as usual, so as not to arouse Bristol's suspicions. We still weren't certain if our young employee was involved in the diamond theft or not, although I suspected she was clueless as to her brother's shenanigans.

Bo reluctantly agreed, but not without first giving me a short lecture on how to have a safe confrontation. After that, he basically threatened to whoop Titan if he didn't keep me safe.

When Titan got off the call, we exchanged a look.

"Your brother's a regular force of nature," Titan said. "He's had my back more times than I care to count, and I know he'll never let me down. Don't worry, I'll do the same for him." Titan shoved his hand into his hoodie pocket, where he'd stashed the honey mustard packets. "Oh—before we head to the cemetery, I need to leave the diamonds at one of our dropoff points in town." He grinned when he saw the curious look on my face.

"No, you don't need to know where it is. Also, unless you have some extra honey mustard packets lying around, I'm going to pick up five that look like these."

"I don't," I said, feeling a little deflated that he wouldn't let me in on the super-secret FBI dropoff point. "That's a good plan. In the meantime, I'm ordering pizza because I'm starving. What kind do you like?"

"I'm a fan of bacon on everything," he said. "And whatever veggies you want, because I like them all."

"You must've been a delight to your mother. I'm a little more picky with my vegetables of choice. Bacon and mushroom pizza it is, then."

As Titan gave Coal another pat and headed out, it hit me that I always felt comfortable with him. Once the door closed, I asked Coal, "You really like him, too, don't you?"

Coal walked over and bumped against my hand. I grabbed my phone and called the pizza place, glad to get some fortification before this uncertain endeavor. Titan had briefed me as to my role at the cemetery. He planned to hide behind the mausoleum and wait until Ethan was close enough to snap the handcuffs on him. My job was to keep Ethan talking and try to fool him with the honey mustard packets.

I felt like a jerk for setting a teen up on a sting like this, but he'd basically set *himself* up for some serious repercussions. It was probably going to break his mama's heart, but I felt pretty certain the feds would go easier on him, given his age.

Plus, it was safer for him *not* to have the diamonds, in case Anne Moreau was sniffing around.

Titan hadn't given me any instructions as to how to trap Anne, but I knew we'd have to deal with that as soon as things were squared away with Ethan. It gave me the creeps that she actually knew my cell number, which I'd recently changed after her husband had left me an ominous voicemail a few months ago. Of course, they were both trying to rattle me—probably because my brother was the only DEA agent who'd gotten close to gathering any kind of evidence that could send Moreau to prison. But why the criminal couple still had bees in their bonnets about Bo, when he'd obviously failed and moved across the country to start an entirely new business, I didn't understand.

The pizza arrived, and I didn't have the willpower to wait for Titan to get back. I dug in, savoring the smoky bacon flavor. Coal licked his lips and gave a nervous yawn. I'd forgotten how irresistible he found pizza.

"Just a tiny piece," I said, hating to break my no human food rule, but understanding just how good this particular pizza smelled. I headed over to drop it in his bowl, but he stuck out his tongue and caught it on the way down, like a kid catching a snowflake.

The doorbell rang, and I took a big bite of pizza before walking over to open it. Titan brandished a handful of honey mustard packets. "Here are your fakes," he said, walking in and pulling his boots off.

"Pizza's here." I grabbed a napkin and wiped my mouth. "I saved you a couple pieces," I joked.

He didn't catch it. Maybe he really believed I could eat six pieces of pizza all by myself. I snickered.

He seemed distracted by his thoughts. "Thanks. Listen, are you sure you're okay with doing this? I could just go over myself and nab Ethan in his car. The only thing holding me back is that I'd like to see how Bristol's involved, if at all. But that will likely come out when they're both questioned, anyway."

"I'm sure Ethan's not dangerous," I said. "And I want to know about Bristol, too."

Titan grabbed a plate and opened the pizza box. "Okay, if you're sure. Wow, this looks great. And I see you left me more than two pieces." He winked as he took a bite. "Now, it's time to gear up."

23

WHEN TITAN SAID "GEAR UP," he wasn't kidding. First, he made sure my phone was able to record, then he placed a practically invisible earpiece in my left ear. We practiced with it a little, and he was able to hear me from upstairs.

Finally, he double checked his handgun before sliding it back in his belt holster. He had the handcuffs handy in his back jeans pocket.

"We're ready," he said.

We wanted to get there before six so Titan could get into position. When we arrived, it had already gotten dark, but the cemetery lights were numerous and bright. Leaving my car parked where Ethan couldn't miss it, we hurried over to the mausoleum. Titan walked around to the back of it, while I positioned myself out front, fiddling with my earpiece until Titan politely asked me to stop.

It was good we'd arrived way ahead of time, because in true West Virginia fashion, Ethan and Bristol showed up early, too.

Standing in front of the mausoleum, I watched as the

brother and sister duo walked my way. Did this mean Bristol knew what was going on?

As they entered the cemetery, Ethan stopped short and placed a hand on Bristol's arm. He said something to her, then she looked around and walked over to a bench and sat down. He must've asked for some privacy. I could tell from the confused look on Bristol's face that she didn't get why her brother wanted to talk to her boss alone. This boded well for her.

As Ethan approached, his walk was a little wobbly. I felt like someone kicked me in the gut. The kid was sick, for the love of everything.

"Hi," he said, his big brown eyes reminding me of his mom. "Did you find them?"

"I did," I said. I nodded toward Bristol. "Does she know what you're doing here?"

He glanced back. "Bristol? No way. She'd kick my butt."

I let out a breath. "So you said you're going to sell these? That can't be easy since cops are looking for them."

"I had a buyer lined up beforehand. And trust me, this buyer is very discreet," he said, stepping closer. "Where are they?"

I unclenched my fists, revealing five honey mustard packets. "Hang on. You said you were using these to help your family. What do you mean?"

"I'm going to buy myself a kidney transplant, so that'll take that burden off my mom. Then I'm going to pay off our house so Mom and Bristol don't have to work unless they want to. They deserve a life that doesn't revolve around me. And Uncle Clark will have hospital bills now, so I'll cover those, too."

"These are blood diamonds, you know. That means people were killed for them, Ethan."

His face crumpled. "I know—it was in those secret emails to

Les. But I've been thinking, and the way I see it, these diamonds will help save a life, and maybe that'll balance those lives that were lost. I can't go on forever on these cyst-filled kidneys. Mom doesn't think I know my time is limited, but I'm not stupid."

Sympathy flooded over me. Ethan had nothing but good intentions for these diamonds.

Wait—I didn't even *have* the actual diamonds.

"Could I see them now?" he asked, holding his hand out.

"Coming now," a voice said in my ear. It was the first time Titan had spoken, and I gave a little start.

As I was about to hand the stand-in packets over, someone jumped out of a car in the parking lot. The minute I caught sight of the man's long blond hair, I shoved Ethan behind me and shouted at Bristol. "Get *down!*"

Lucas Janssen stalked right past Bristol, who had dropped to the ground and was crawling under the bench as fast as she could. He toted what I was pretty sure was an AK-47.

"Get back!" I shouted, feigning bravery. What was I doing? I didn't have a weapon on me.

I could feel Ethan's thin hands pressing into my back as he cowered behind me. I wasn't letting this kid die. The Belgian freak would have to go through me first.

"I've got him." Titan's voice in my earpiece was never more welcome. But what did he *mean*? He had Janssen in his sights? Was I supposed to keep stalling?

Janssen didn't slow at my command. He continued to stride our way, his AK aimed at my chest.

I supposed it was handy that this wasn't the first time someone had pulled a gun on me. I wasn't quite as shaky as I'd been the first time, but this was a much bigger gun, and this dude obviously wasn't planning to monologue. He wanted the diamonds...which I *did not even have.*

"Hand them over," he said, his accent heavier than ever. "She wants what's hers."

She? "You mean you work for Anne Moreau?" I asked.

He didn't budge.

"She sent you," I said.

He thrust his hand out. "Give them to me, *now.*" An evil grin crossed his lips. "Then I'll make sure you die quickly."

I had no alternative. I opened my hand.

A gunshot crack sounded, quickly followed by two more shots, but none of them seemed to hit me. I didn't hesitate. Falling backward, I knocked Ethan onto the knoll behind us. My body covered his. I looked up at the stars. Was this it? I didn't want to think of our bodies getting ripped up by bullets. Bo would be upset.

Titan shouted, "You're okay! Macy, you're okay!"

I lowered my gaze, finally registering what he was saying. I slowly rolled off Ethan before pulling him into a sitting position. He gave a ragged gasp and rubbed at his chest.

I said, "I'm sorry if I hurt you. It was all I could think to do when I heard the gunshots."

"You...saved me," Ethan's voice was croaky.

Still a little dazed, I glanced toward Janssen. The tall man was sprawled on the walkway, completely still. Blood pooled underneath his head and chest, where Titan's bullets had found their mark.

Titan jogged past us to check Janssen. Once he'd felt for a pulse that was obviously not there, he picked up the AK. In a few quick moves, he'd removed the magazine and cleared the chamber.

"*There's* the one you need to thank," I told Ethan. "He saved us."

Titan walked back to us and clamped a strong, steadying hand on my shoulder. "Janssen left me no choice. He would've killed all of you. The Moreaus always clean up after themselves. Thankfully, I got him before he could fire." After lingering for another moment, he headed down to Bristol and helped her to her feet.

"Come back to my place." I spoke gently to Ethan, who was probably in shock. "I'll call your mom."

"I did this," Ethan muttered. "I could've gotten my sister *killed*."

"It didn't happen," I said, scooting closer. "My friend there is with the FBI. You'll just need to tell him the truth, like you told me."

Titan and Bristol walked our way. Bristol's dark hair was disheveled, and her face was flushed with anger. "Ethan, what have you gotten yourself into?"

Ethan walked over and hugged his sister. "I'm so sorry. I never meant for any of this to happen."

Titan came over to my side and gingerly removed my earpiece. His voice was soft. "You did well, Macy. Your brother's going to be proud."

I couldn't help myself. I burst into long-overdue tears.

Titan pulled me into a tight hug. I didn't even reach his shoulders. For someone who'd just shot a man, he was incredibly calm. As my crying abated, I became more than a little aware of the quiet strength of the man holding me. It was the kind of impression I'd never shake.

TITAN CALLED and filled Bo in on our way home, so my brother was pacing by my back gate when we drove up. He rushed to my car door and gave me a long hug. As Titan got out of the driver's seat and stood, Bo's eyes met his. I read every emotion that flitted across my brother's face—anger, relief, and finally, gratefulness. "Thanks," Bo said. His eyes flashed with one final emotion I hadn't seen before—revenge. "I'll be the one calling Anne Moreau," he said. "My sister's out."

Titan gave a respectful dip of his head. Bristol and Ethan emerged from the car and followed us inside. Coal didn't even bark at the crowd coming into his house. He simply sat by the door, his tail wagging as each new visitor entered. I realized he'd met everyone here before. Dogs' sense of smell was not something to be taken lightly, that was for sure.

I glanced at my kitchen counter, where five large take-out cups from Barks & Beans were lined up.

"Chai lattes," Bo explained. "Charity thought they'd be bracing and wouldn't keep you up all night."

"Bless that sweet woman," I said, grabbing a cup and taking a sip. The others did the same.

Ethan practically collapsed onto the couch, and Bristol sat down beside him. "I didn't get the diamonds," he said. "I'm never getting a kidney, sis."

Bristol silently patted his knee. Her dark eyes met my own, and I knew I had to explain.

"I don't have them," I said. "The FBI does." I looked at Titan, who was leaning on the kitchen counter.

"I need to talk to my boss," Titan said. "Just give me a minute. Do you mind if I go in the other room?"

"Of course not."

He walked down the hallway into my guest bedroom.

I flipped on the Christmas tree lights, hoping for a distraction. The cheery glow seemed to brighten the somber mood. Bo settled into a nearby chair. "Have you called Della?" he asked.

"I called from the car. She should get here any minute."

Bristol and Ethan had fallen into a conversation, so I leaned in toward Bo. "What are you going to tell Anne Moreau?" I asked. "It turns out Janssen was her man on the spot. I guess he never left the country."

"He didn't. The FBI just texted me that the man who was traveling with Janssen's passport turned out to be an imposter. Someone who'd been paid to wear a blond wig and stand in for Janssen, not knowing what was waiting on the other end."

I had to give Anne Moreau credit—she was quite the schemer. "She did all this just to get those diamonds?" I asked.

Bo nodded. "That's her thing. Moreau deals in arms and sometimes art, but she deals in jewels—the rarer, the better. Leo usually gets her the gems that she wants, but I guess she must've decided to handle this one on her own. She has enough connections in our part of West Virginia, which explains why she chose this area for her smuggling operation."

Titan walked back into the room. "She's getting more independent, and that's not a good thing," he said. He turned to Ethan and Bristol, who had fallen silent. "I've talked with my boss, and he's inclined to follow my suggestion."

The siblings waited in silence, gripping their cups of tea. Two sets of brown eyes watched for Titan to speak again.

"See, we're all pretty impressed that you were able to hack into the dark web so easily...much less intercept a diamond shipment," Titan continued. "Not that we condone your actions, of course. But if you'd be willing to go through training and eventually come to work for us, we'd be able to overlook this incident *and* there might be a way to pull some strings for a transplant. After all, the FBI would want you around for a good long time."

I could've hugged Titan. Instead, I just gazed up at him like a daft fool.

Bristol gave a little squeal. "Thank you, sir. You won't regret it. My brother is one of the smartest people I know."

Ethan stood, and with a serious look, he walked over to

Titan and shook his hand. "I'm sorry for what I put everyone through. I'll need to talk with my mom, but I think this could work out."

The doorbell rang, so I hopped up to open it. Della stood outside, her eyes anxious. "Are the kids okay?"

"They definitely are. You don't have to worry," I said. And if that transplant really did come through, one of Della's biggest worries was about to disappear.

24

It wasn't until I'd tucked into bed at eleven that I realized I'd totally stood Summer up. I sent her a frantic text, telling her I was sorry for contacting her so late, but something had come up, so I didn't have time to let her know first.

My phone rang as I was mid-text. Summer was on the other end.

"Girl! What happened?" she asked.

"I thought you were early to bed and early to rise," I said. "I don't want to keep you up."

"It doesn't matter tonight. Guess who's at my house getting all the kitties riled up?"

"Uh-oh. Not—"

"Waffles," she finished. "You guessed it. They called after closing time, so I had to let them drop her off here."

"Oh, I'm so sorry," I said. I wasn't sure who I was more sorry for, the unwanted Labradoodle or Summer, who had to keep taking her in.

"You might as well explain yourself," she continued.

"Alright, but you'd better settle in, because this story is a real doozy."

"I'd expect nothing less from you," Summer said.

THE NEXT MORNING, as discussed, I headed over to Bo's house, where Titan was waiting, his recording equipment already set up. Stormy had been placed in her kitty crate in the bathroom, where she was giving the occasional forlorn cry.

There was only one loose end left, and that was to place a call to Anne Louise Moreau.

Of course, Bo wasn't about to let me call her back, but I'd convinced him to let me come over and listen in, since he knew I'd get all the details of the conversation out of him sooner or later.

I wasn't quite sure what tack my brother was going to take, but I knew for certain it wouldn't involve idle threats. If Bo made a threat, he'd follow up on it—all the more reason for me to be privy to things today, in case I needed to beg him to back down later.

After having a deep conversation with Titan, who looked like he hadn't gotten much sleep, Bo took my phone and placed the call. We heard it ring a couple of times through our speakers, then I recognized the southern drawl of the woman who'd called me before.

"Aw, honey. I'm *so* sorry my man gave you such a hard time. But I heard you got those diamonds in the end. Were you calling to make a deal?"

Bo's face was a mask of suppressed fury. "Hello, Anne Louise," he said. "You might've heard of me. I'm Macy's brother, Bo."

The drawl turned almost sultry. "Why, Boaz Hatfield, why're you calling little ol' me?"

"I'm calling because you nearly killed my sister. I'm calling because you'll never get your hands on those diamonds." He gave a slight pause. Like some kind of superhero, he seemed to be harnessing his energy before exploding with power. "I'm calling to tell you that if you contact my sister again, *I'm going to blow your husband's operation sky-high.*"

Titan shook his head. Apparently this was *not* part of the script.

Her voice roughened. "Darlin', I hate to break it to you, but that isn't really a threat. In fact, I'll be contactin' you again so we can talk more about what you can do for me in that regard. But don't you fret. I'll leave your sister alone. *You're* the one I want." She hung up.

Titan slammed down his headphones and marched over to Bo. "What was that?"

Bo shrugged. "Just putting a little scare into her."

"You don't taunt someone like Anne Moreau," Titan said. I had to agree with him.

"Doesn't matter," Bo said, handing my phone back. "I guess you could say we ended things amicably."

"Whatever *amicably* means for Anne Louise," Titan said. "We'll talk more later. I have to pick up the diamonds and get back to headquarters." He started packing up his equipment.

"I understand." Bo didn't appear to be the least bit remorseful.

Things were obviously strained between the two men, so I stood. "I'll get back home now. But Titan, thank you again for creating a job for Ethan—and for giving his family hope." I strode over and gave him a quick hug that wouldn't raise Bo's eyebrows. "And thank you again for saving our lives," I added.

I was relieved when Titan gave me a warm response. "I was

happy to, Macy. I don't want to think what could've happened if you'd gone to meet Ethan alone."

"There's no way we could've known Janssen was still around, following me," I said.

Titan shook his head. "I should've been more observant and guessed the flight to Belgium was a ruse."

Bo seemed to snap out of his funk. "You came through for my sister. Don't beat yourself up."

Sensing that Bo and Titan were about to make amends, I said goodbye and slipped outside. As snowflakes started dusting the sidewalk, I felt an immense sense of relief, like I could finally get in the holiday spirit. "Girl's Day Out shopping, here I come," I said, doing a little twirl.

Girl's Day Out came and went with a bang. Not only did we get several pet foster families lined up, but we also gained quite a few new customers who fell for Kylie's foam art coffee drinks. They swore to return, bringing all their friends with them.

Della invited Bo and me over to join their family for a meal. Clark sat at the table, looking hale and hearty as ever.

"It's good to see you with your color back," I said. "We visited you in the hospital quite a few times."

"I heard," Clark said. "So Les was trying to spy on me, was he? He thought I had the diamonds?"

"That was the thing," I said, sitting down next to him. "No one knew *who* had them. Les suspected you of somehow stealing them before the grenade launcher holdup. We're not sure what he told Janssen in the trailer—if he told him anything. But for some reason, Janssen killed him. Maybe just because, like my FBI friend said, his boss always makes sure to clean up loose ends."

"It's sad," Della said, placing a spiral ham on the table. "I mean, I didn't like Les much, but he didn't deserve to die that way."

"Well, he was the one who set up the entire thing," Ethan said. He seemed to have grown wiser over the past week.

"One thing I don't understand is that Christian Gill's name was on the safe deposit lockbox where the diamonds were stored," I mused.

"What?" Della looked up sharply.

"I'm sorry. I didn't tell you because I knew you cared for him," I said.

Bo coated his salad with dressing. "I'll tell you why," he said. "Les and John Wright decided to use that lockbox so Christian would be incriminated if anything went wrong. As a banker, Wright had access to it, so he just decided to hide them there. He flat out lied that he didn't see the person who deposited the diamonds in it."

"So Christian wasn't involved at all?" Della asked.

"Not a bit," Bo said, bringing a forkful to his mouth.

"But what about the money?" Bristol said. "I mean, I know the diamonds were worth a lot more, but half a million dollars is nothing to sneeze at."

"No, it's not," Clark said. "You know, I only remember bits and pieces of the day of the wreck. I remember seeing you in the cafe that morning, Bristol. Then I remember the man with the grenade launcher. I can't really remember hitting the ice, though."

"Someone used a payphone near Barks & Beans to tell emergency services about the wreck," I said. "I've wondered if it was the same person who took the money. Do you remember seeing anyone else that day?"

Clark got a dreamy look in his eyes. "I saw an angel," he said slowly.

Della sat up straighter. "What? You didn't tell me this."

"I think I was halfway between heaven and earth when this angel with a cloud of black hair and pure white skin came down. She was holding my arm, then she disappeared. I know it sounds kooky, but I swear I saw her."

Clark's story didn't seem so far-fetched to me. In fact, he seemed to be describing none other than Sheldia Powers, the librarian.

AFTER FLOATING my theory past Bo on the way home, he agreed I should let Detective Hatcher know what Clark had said. He could at least check into Sheldia's bank records and make sure there had been no huge monetary deposits after Black Friday.

The next day the detective called me back, assuring me Sheldia's accounts were normal. Clark must've imagined the angel, which wasn't uncommon for those hovering near death, he said.

But that weekend, when I was visiting Dylan in his art gallery, a white, rusty minivan pulled up and parked on the opposite side of the street. Sheldia got out of the driver's side, then opened the sliding door to help a young boy out of his brand-new carseat. She must've gotten the call for her first foster child. I watched them walk hand-in-hand down the sidewalk and turn into a toy shop. Sheldia Powers, the woman who'd had a terrible childhood, had finally gotten what she wanted—a new Bookmobile bus, backpacks for foster kids, and the opportunity to pour some of herself into foster children.

If she did take that money, I didn't ever want to know.

You can now preorder Heather Day Gilbert's next Barks & Beans Cafe cozy mystery,

FAIR TRADE

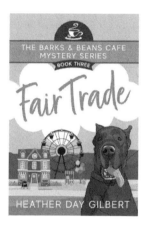

Welcome to the Barks & Beans Cafe, a quaint place where folks pet shelter dogs while enjoying a cup of java…and where murder sometimes pays a visit.

With the one-year anniversary of the now-successful Barks & Beans Cafe approaching, siblings Macy and Bo Hatfield set up an iced coffee booth at the state fair. Taking a break from brewing, Macy bumps into Carolina, a long-lost childhood friend who's now sitting pretty as a country superstar. Macy tries not to fangirl too hard when her old friend extends an invitation to meet the rest of the Carolina Crush band before their opening show.

But when Carolina falls victim to not one, but two near-death experiences, Macy takes it upon herself to find out who has it in for her old friend. Fortified with plenty of roasted corn, cinnamon rolls, and her brother's signature iced maple latte, Macy takes to the Ferris wheel to get the lay of the land from the air. She discovers too late that this year's fair isn't all fun and games...but she's already locked in for the ride.

Join siblings Macy and Bo Hatfield as they sniff out crimes in their hometown...with plenty of dogs along for the ride! The Barks & Beans Cafe cozy mystery series features a small town, an amateur sleuth, and no swearing or graphic scenes. Find all the books at heatherdaygilbert.com!

ALSO BY HEATHER DAY GILBERT

The Barks & Beans Cafe cozy mystery series in order:

Book 1: No Filter

Book 2: Iced Over

Book 3: Fair Trade

Be sure to sign up now for Heather's newsletter at heatherdaygilbert.com for updates, special deals, & giveaways!

And if you enjoyed this book, please be sure to leave a review at online book retailers and tell your friends! Thank you!

Printed in Great Britain
by Amazon

51659069R00128